Write On,
Callie Jones

NAOMI ZUCKER

EGMONT
USA
NEW YORK

EGMONT

We bring stories to life

First published by Egmont USA, 2010
443 Park Avenue South, Suite 806
New York, NY 10016

1 3 5 7 9 8 6 4 2

www.egmontusa.com
www.naomizucker.net

Library of Congress Cataloging-in-Publication Data

Zucker, Naomi Flink.
Write on, Callie Jones / by Naomi Zucker.
p. cm.
Summary: As she continues to establish rules for navigating middle school, aspiring author
Callie writes for the school newspaper until the principal cancels her article and Callie's
quest to have her voice heard leads to a series of unexpected consequences.
ISBN 978-1-60684-028-3 (hardcover)
[1. Newspapers—Fiction. 2. Authorship—Fiction. 3. Rules (Philosophy)—Fiction.
4. Middle schools—Fiction. 5. Schools—Fiction.] I. Title.
PZ7.Z7795Wr 2010
[Fic]—dc22
2010023134

Printed in the United States of America

CPSIA tracking label information:
Random House Production • 1745 Broadway • New York, NY 10019

For Norman, at 50.

●　●　●　●　●

1 C. X. Jones, Star Reporter

On Tuesday, January 8, at two thirty in the afternoon, as the girls' hockey team was changing in the locker room, an enormous cockroach crawled out of Sophia Meyer's shorts. Sophia screamed loudly. Hearing her screams, and fearing the worst, a male teacher ran in from the hallway. The girls took cover behind locker doors and on top of benches. The invading culprit escaped through a crack in the wall and was not seen again.

When questioned afterward, Sophia exclaimed, "It was the ugliest, slimiest thing I've ever seen in my life! I was terrified." Marianne Stoddard, who was in the locker room when the teacher burst in, says that she "will never get undressed in the locker room again. Not ever. Even if I get thrown off the team."

The male teacher, when interviewed, said he preferred not to discuss what happened and requested that his name not be used.

Buzz Henwick, the school custodian, reports that an exterminator has been called in to spray the locker room, and added, "The little buggers are done for."

All involved hope that the unfortunate incident will not be repeated.

That's the story I wrote for our new middle-school newspaper. Or what I hope will be in our school paper. And what I hope will be my first published story. Because I want to be a writer. Someday. But when you're in sixth grade, and a girl, wanting to be a writer isn't something you tell people. Not when you're already tiptoeing over a very narrow, very shaky bridge between "weird" and "nerd." And trying very hard not to fall into either swamp.

Popular girls draw fashion designs in their

notebooks. Or wedding dresses. Then they show them to their friends. I write stories in my notebook. And I never show them to anyone. Because if you tell someone that you write stories . . . Forget "weird." You're way past "nerd." You are irrevocably, irretrievably, irreversibly invisible. Forever. Or until you graduate from school. Which will seem like forever.

It's okay that I don't show my stories to anybody. And it's okay that I'm not one of the popular girls. Really. It is. I don't ever want to be like them, the way they whisper and stare and act as though everything they tell each other is the most exciting news in the world. When mostly what they're telling each other is some slimy gossip. But the thing is they're always together. They sit together at lunch, and they walk down the hall with their arms around each other. They've got a group. And that's what I want. A group.

You wouldn't think a girl with six brothers and sisters and who hasn't even got her own room and has to share with her younger sister would want a group. But I do.

I've got a best friend, Alyce, but together there's

just the two of us. That's not a group. If Alyce is home sick or has a different lunch period or has to go somewhere after school, then it's just me. Alone. Hoping not to get to school too early so I won't have to wait outside alone. Skipping lunch so I won't have to eat alone. Walking home alone with no one to talk to. So I really want a group.

I didn't think I'd ever find one. Until last Tuesday, when Shane Belcher caught up to me on the way into school and said, "Cal, are you going to join the new school newspaper? The first meeting's this afternoon."

A newspaper. I could write stuff. And that wouldn't be weird. And there'd be other kids writing stuff, too. We could be a group. If a fairy godmother had offered me three wishes, those would have been two of them—me writing and being in a group.

Shane's smirking! He knew about the newspaper, and I didn't. My third wish, getting back to that fairy godmother, would probably have been for Shane, right at that moment, to turn into a frog. And no way would I ever have kissed him.

So I put on my Egyptian mummy face, the one

I use when my parents say, "Callie, we need to talk," and I say, "The newspaper, Shane? Of course I'm going. What, did you think you were the only person who can write for the newspaper?"

"Write for what newspaper, Callie?"

Alyce has just come up behind me.

"The new school newspaper. The first meeting is this afternoon."

"Oh, Callie. I'll come with you. I bet we could write something together."

Great, just great. I hadn't even become a reporter and I've already got another name next to mine under the headline. My name! I needed to decide what my reporter name was going to be. Not Callie Jones—too much of a kid's name. Well, I am a kid, but my real name, Calliope Jones, is just bizarre. C. Jones? No, that sounded like a name for a bank teller.

I was wishing I had a middle name, so I could use two initials, when it came to me—C. X. Jones. Perfect. *X* for unknown quantity. Reporter C. X. Jones—no one knows where she'll turn up or what she'll be asking. C. X. Jones didn't walk, she dashed; she didn't ask questions, she shot them out like bullets. C. X. Jones was one tough reporter.

But for now, I was still plain old Callie Jones. And, at two thirty on Tuesday afternoon, I wasn't dashing or questioning; I was sitting at a desk in room 214 of Hillcrest Middle School. Next to me, Alyce was chattering about something. I hoped we wouldn't be the only two kids who showed up. We weren't exactly a group. Or maybe this was one of Shane's twisted jokes. Did he make up this whole thing about a newspaper and a meeting just so he could be standing outside, waiting for me, laughing at me?

Then a girl opened the door a quarter of the way and peered inside.

"Is this where the newspaper is supposed to meet?"

Okay, Shane, you've escaped my wrath—for now.

The girl edged her way around the door and shut it behind her. Softly. She sat down three seats back from us.

Alyce turned around and said, "Hi, my name's Alyce. With a *y*." Alyce is never at a loss for words.

The girl looked at me. "Jamie?"

Was she asking if my name was Jamie? Did I look like someone else?

While I was trying to figure that one out, Alyce took over.

"Hi, Jamie. This is Callie."

"Hi, Callie?"

I finally got it—Jamie always ended her sentences with question marks. I wondered how she talked when she was *really* asking a question.

More kids were coming in. A small, skinny boy, wearing a really cool hat, was next. The kid wasn't wearing a baseball hat, like every other boy in the entire country. His hat had a wide brim that curled up on the sides, with a leather band around it. It took guts to wear a hat like that, but just the same, it really was cool. Right behind the hat kid, almost as if he were glued to his back, was a bigger kid who looked like the turkey balloon in the Thanksgiving parade—with a round body and short little legs. The hat kid didn't look at anybody, just moved to a desk, with the turkey right behind him.

"Hey, Elwin," the turkey said. "Is this where you hang out? With the girls?"

The kid named Elwin slid into a seat and, not

looking at the turkey, shot back, "Shut up, Junior. Don't you have to go kill some cats?"

Alyce made a feeble screech. She can be quite literal sometimes.

The kid named Junior snatched Elwin's hat and said, "You're right, midget. I don't bother with mice."

Elwin tried to grab his hat back, but the turkey was already halfway to the door. I really felt sorry for Elwin. The hat was cool—and different. Without it, he was only a small, skinny kid.

Just as Junior reached the door, Shane walked in with a few other kids. Junior threw Elwin's hat back at him. Elwin grabbed for it, missed, and picked it up off the floor.

One of the new kids headed for the teacher's desk and sat down behind it. He took off his baseball cap, folded the back of it under, put it on again like a visor, slammed his feet up on the desk, and announced, grinning, "Okay, reporters, let's get started."

A bunch more kids were coming in and one of them called out, "Get up, Andrik. I just saw the teacher heading down the hall."

Andrik jackknifed out of the teacher's chair and strolled to a desk.

I did want to be part of a group, but I was having doubts about this one. I mean, look at who was there—a loudmouth, a kid who got bullied, a girl who turned her own name into a question, and Alyce with a *y*. Alyce is my best friend, which tells you something about *her* status. And then there was Shane. Shane didn't really fit in this crazy-quilt group. Or maybe he did. Shane is really smart—all As, so teachers really like him. But the weird thing is that the popular kids like him anyway. Everybody likes him. After school, he shoots hoops with the dump rats. Shane could be a group all by himself.

This was all getting to be much too confusing. Other people always seem to know the rules, while I'm still trying to figure them out. So when I finally catch on to a rule, I write it down. Like this one:

Callie's Rule:

• A bunch is not a group.

And that's what we all were, a bunch of kids, not a group, sitting together in a room, waiting for something to happen. And then something did happen—or actually, someone.

"Hello. And welcome. I'm glad to see so many of you here. I'm Mr. Fischer."

Whoa, Callie! Breathe, I told myself. Okay, now take another breath. That's it. Just keep breathing. But it really was hard to breathe and look at Mr. Fischer at the same time.

Mr. Fischer had curly black hair and deep blue eyes, and he looked like a movie star. Mr. Fischer moved to the front of the teacher's desk and half sat on it, one leg on the floor, the other leg dangling. When he smiled, his eyes crinkled at the corners. I thought I felt a crinkle in my chest. Mr. Fischer couldn't be a teacher.

"Some of you know me from seventh-grade English."

He *was* a teacher. Right here in this school. The crinkle was turning into a crimp. But—groan—there were eight whole months before I'd be in seventh grade. And—double groan—then I still might get a different English teacher. Hold on, Callie, I thought. Forget about seventh grade. Mr. Fischer was right there, right then, right in front of me.

Alyce poked me in the back.

"Oh, Callie, he is *so* adorable."

"Alyce, he'll hear you!"

"It seems . . ." When Mr. Fischer was speaking, his voice made me feel all bright and warm, as though a hundred candles had been lit inside me.

"It seems," Mr. Fischer was saying in his warm-candle voice, "I'm to be the adviser for the new student newspaper. I know you've had a long day in school, so let's get started. The first order of business ought to be to give this paper a name. Any suggestions?"

Kids started to call out names—really boring names—but Mr. Fischer asked one of the kids to write them all on the board. *The Hillcrest Herald. The Post. The Courier. The Paper (Not Plastic).* That last one was Andrik's suggestion. Okay, I had to admit it was pretty funny, but a newspaper is not a comic book.

I had to come up with a name, a really good one, the best name that anyone, even Mr. Fischer, could ever imagine. I was thinking as hard as I could, and then . . . My parents always tell me that I have to take my time before I speak; my mother says to install a pause button in my mouth. Well, I was thinking, but then an idea popped into my brain, and, before I could press pause, my mouth was speaking.

"Mr. Fischer?"

Mr. Fischer looked at me, right straight at me, and asked me my name. I felt as though a flock of birds had fluttered into my throat. If I tried to talk, I'd chirp.

"C-Callie. Jones," I chirped.

"Yes, Callie Jones, have you a suggestion?"

I heard my brain grumbling, something about what good was a pause button if I was never going to use it anyway. But Mr. Fischer was looking at me, waiting for me to say something. I had to just go ahead and say it.

"Mr. Fischer, what about calling the paper *The Hawk*? Because . . . because a hawk circles around . . . looking all around . . . and when he spots something interesting, he swoops down and catches it . . . like what a really good newspaper does."

I couldn't believe I'd said all of that. It was crazy. My idea was just crazy. Everyone was staring at me. And Mr. Fischer wasn't saying a word, just looking at me.

"That's not a bad idea. Not bad at all. Let's

write that down and then, if there are no other suggestions, we'll take a vote."

Not bad! He said my idea was not bad! He liked it. I didn't care if not one other person in the whole room voted for my name. Mr. Fischer liked it!

What happened next was even better. Well, almost better. When we voted, everyone who suggested a name voted for their own. But everyone else—and here's the almost better part—every other single person in the entire room voted for *The Hawk*. My name won. People voted for me, for my idea. I was almost like a member of the group.

"Well, it looks as if our newspaper has a name, *The Hawk*."

Mr. Fischer smiled at me. He looked right straight at me and smiled.

I feel some more rules coming on.

Callie's Rules About Ideas:

- Boring ideas go on the whiteboard.
- Crazy ideas—no, brilliant ideas—go from the white board to the front page, right at the top.

- The best ideas—the super-best,
  most brilliant of all ideas—are the ones
  that pop right up like rabbits
  in a shooting gallery. Hit one of those
  ideas, and you win the prize.

After we'd chosen a name—my name—Mr. Fischer told us what *The Hawk* (ta-da!) was going to look like. After the first issue, Mr. Fischer said, he wanted the paper to have four pages. The first page would be school news; the second would have important announcements, cafeteria menus, sports schedules—the boring stuff. The third page—and this was where I really got interested—the third page, Mr. Fischer said, would be the editorial page, where the newspaper writers got to express their opinions about school matters and other students had their letters printed. I stopped listening when Mr. Fischer talked about the fourth page. I think it was something about school sports. It was that third page I cared about. There're two things I know I'm good at—writing and having opinions. And if I could get to write about my opinions, well, then I'd be twice as good.

I was trying to decide which of my opinions I should write about, when Mr. Fischer started to talk about the future of newspapers.

"People," Mr. Fischer said, "are predicting the death of newspapers. Who would want to read the news on paper when they could get all their news electronically? Who knows? By the time you grow up, you might even be getting your morning news stories from your bathroom mirrors." His eyes crinkled again. "But until that time comes, we've still got newspapers—on paper—and that's what we're all going to be working on."

Mr. Fischer gave us some rules for writing news stories—I wrote down every word—and then he said, "Now I'm going to give you your first assignments. I'd like each of you to write a brief news story."

Write a story. A story that Mr. Fischer was going to read. I knew right then that I had to write the best story he'd ever read.

"Your story," Mr. Fischer said, "must be factual, and it must concern something that happened here at school."

Right here at school. Okay, so I don't have to

go skulking around corners or start hanging out at the police station.

"And, of course," he said, "I want you to follow the rules I set out for you this afternoon. These stories won't all be perfect, but the more you practice, the better you'll get. Send your stories to my email."

Mr. Fischer wrote his email address on the board. I engraved it in my memory.

"Your deadline—another term you're going to be hearing—will be next Monday. I'll read through your stories, and we'll meet here again in a week."

All the kids were getting ready to leave, stuffing their notebooks and pencils into their backpacks. I stayed in my seat, wringing out my brain for a question that I could go up and ask Mr. Fischer— something really smart, but casual, like I just happened to think of it as I walked by. Although I'd have the question all worked out and memorized. This time I really was going to put my mouth on pause—plan the whole thing out in my brain before I opened my mouth. But my brain was dry, arid, like the Sahara Desert, and I couldn't squeeze out a single drop of an idea.

It didn't matter, because just then Mr. Nolan walked into the room. Mr. Nolan's the principal, and he doesn't actually walk. Mr. Nolan is unbelievably tall and skinny, and he moves as if he's wearing stilts—you know, the way a stilt walker has to lift his knees really high and then stretch out one long stilt in front of him.

"Would you all take your seats, please?"

Everyone sat back down. Everyone but me. I was already sitting but trying to shrink down as far as I could in my seat, hoping Mr. Nolan wouldn't see me. Last year, I'd sort of had a problem with Mr. Nolan. But it's not just me. Everyone in school calls him Mr. No-Man. That's because whenever you ask him anything, he always says no.

Why did Mr. No-Man have to parade himself in here today? My brain was wrung dry before, but with Mr. No-Man there, I practically went into brain arrest. I knew I'd never be able to think of a question for Mr. Fischer.

"I'm glad to see so many of you here today." Mr. No-Man has a voice that makes you feel all cold and shivery. "As you know, this will be the first newspaper for Hillcrest Middle School. I'm sure

Mr. Fischer has already talked to you about how this newspaper must be something that we can all be proud of."

We? What did that Negative Number mean by "we"? He wasn't going to be the newspaper adviser. I hoped. He wouldn't, would he?

"Now, this will be your first experience writing something that will actually be published, and it is of the utmost importance that everything that is published, that appears in our newspaper, represents the best, and only the best, aspects of our school. Therefore, I have instructed Mr. Fischer that I would like to review each issue of the paper before it is printed. I do not intend to correct your articles; that will be Mr. Fischer's job. My job will be simply to make sure that nothing . . . Let's just say that I want nothing inappropriate to appear in the Hillcrest Middle School newspaper."

Oh no! Mr. No-Man was going to ruin everything. The only reason Mr. No-Man wanted to check over the paper was so he could say no. And he'd certainly say no to any story that had my name at the top of it. "No, Calliope, you may not publish this article. It is inappropriate."

I started thinking—not talking, just thinking, no need for the pause button. I was thinking that maybe I should just quit the paper right away. Stand up and walk out of the room. Sort of the opposite of a sit-in—a walkout.

Right. That'd look good. Not say anything, stand up, and walk out. Like I had to go to the girls' room or something.

All the while the No-Man was speaking, Mr. Fischer never said a word. He didn't nod or smile. When the No-Man was finished, Mr. Fischer didn't even say thank you to him. Mr. Fischer clearly didn't like the No-Man any more than I did. I smiled a small, knowing smile that would tell him we were both thinking the same thing, and tried to catch his eye, but Mr. Fischer didn't look my way. My smile slowly faded.

But that was okay. As I left the room, I knew that I was going to write a really important story. I'd walk into room 214 . . . No, not walk. I'd glide in, all confident. Mr. Fischer would be perched on the edge of the desk, with one leg dangling, and he'd turn to me and smile that crinkly smile of his, and he'd say . . .

Okay, what would he say?

Got it. He'd say, "Hi, Callie. I see you've got a story for me. I hope it's as good as your idea for naming the paper."

And I'd just hand him my story and not say a word, so as not to seem too full of myself.

As Mr. Fischer is reading my story, he stops every once in a while, looks up at me, and says, "This is really good," or "I really like this part." Stuff like that. When he's finished, he puts down my story, looks right at me, and says, "Callie, this may well be the best story any middle-school student has ever written. It's going to go right on the front page of the first edition of *The Hawk*. Callie, I know you're going to have a great future as a reporter."

So there I was, my head deep in fantasyland, when I walked smack into a bunch of girls yapping like puppies in a pet shop. They'd just reported the cockroach incident and were still talking about it. Flashbulbs! Fantasy out, reality in. I whipped out my pencil and notebook and began interviewing witnesses. This story was so easy—I had all the facts and most of the people involved right there. Even the teacher who'd walked in on them. All I had to do was talk to the janitor, and then I'd be done.

Not quite. Just then, the Negative Number came out of his office.

"Girls," he said, "I've just been informed about the incident in the girls' locker room. Now, I can see that you girls are quite upset, but I think you may be overreacting. I'm certain that what you saw was not a cockroach but a harmless water bug. Those things tend to appear wherever there is water—around showers, sinks. But we would never, I repeat, *never* have cockroaches in this school.

"So I think you should all just calm down now and go on home. We'll have the exterminator here tonight, and there will not be any more water bugs."

He stopped and looked at each of the girls, as if daring them to say the bug was really a cockroach.

"There will not be water bugs or bugs of any sort in this school when you come back in the morning."

Nice try, Mr. Nolan. But when I wrote my story, it was going to be a cockroach. That's what the girls thought it was, that's what they said it was, and that's how I was going to report it.

So here I am, sitting at our dining room table, trying to type on my brother's laptop, while the twins forage around my feet for a missing action figure, my brother Jack keeps asking me how much longer I'll be needing his computer, and my sister Andy suddenly shoves her fingers in front of my face to ask what I think of her new burnt-sienna nail polish and would I like her to do my nails in the same color.

"Fred," Ted says, "you got any gum left?"

"Just the piece from last night. I saved it."

"You did? Where?"

"I put it in my hair."

Everyone—Ted, Jack, Andy, and even me— looks at Fred. Then Andy picks up her manicure scissors and says, "Looks like you'll be getting a Mohawk, little man. Now, hold still."

"Boys," I say, kicking the toy robot out from under the table, "take this stupid thing away and let me work. Jack, if you don't stop interrupting me, I'll be here all night, and you'll never get your laptop back. And Andy, if you paint my nails, I won't be able to type. So would all of you please clear out and let me work?"

Amazing! They all leave. It must have been my C. X. Jones personality that convinced them.

I really like this story. All the while I've been writing, I've felt as light as a snowflake, as if I could float through the air. I'm about to press the send button, but then I decide to read it over. I want to see my story the way Mr. Fischer will see it, reading it for the first time. But when I read my story in Mr. Fischer mode, I thud to the ground like a chunk of ice sliding off the roof. My story has to be the most ridiculous thing anyone ever wrote. A news story about a cockroach? Disgusting. And what about all those girls undressing in the locker room when a man walks in? Maybe that isn't something that should go into a school paper.

Mr. Fischer will never say that my story is utterly repulsive. He'll say something tactful, like, "Interesting story, Callie, but not quite what I was looking for."

But what if he decides to read the cockroach story aloud to everyone? As an example of a totally inappropriate news story. Then what? They'll all laugh, of course. And Mr. Fischer will laugh with them. And what do I do then? Pretend to laugh with them? As if I'd meant the whole thing as a joke all along?

Okay, Callie. Hit the delete key. But I can't delete it. The stupid cockroach story is all I've got. It's either the cockroach story or nothing. And nothing means just that—no story, no future as a reporter for *The Hawk*, no Mr. Fischer. Not now, not ever. So I guess it'll have to be the cockroach story.

My hands shake as I push the cursor toward send. Then I pull it back. I need a new story, a serious story, a really important story. But I haven't got a new story, and there's no more time. Today's Monday, the last day to submit. If I don't submit the cockroach story, I'm finished. No story, no newspaper, no group. But if I do submit it, I'll be finished anyway.

Either way, I'm finished. I hit send.

Well, it's done. There's no backing out now. If everyone laughs at me, I promise, I'll never write another thing. Maybe I could study cosmetology. At that school that advertises on TV. There's always a demand for nail polish.

2 Cockroaches and Chaos

There are a lot fewer kids in the room for the second meeting. I guess some of them couldn't find a good story to write. Or maybe they just had better sense than I did. What was I thinking? A story about a cockroach?

I do know a few of the kids from the first meeting. There's Jamie, the girl who even says her own name like a question, sitting over by the window. Andrik is writing a fake assignment on the board. And Elwin's sitting up front—no Junior, though. I'm glad about that. I was sort of worried that Junior might decide to tail Elwin to every meeting, maybe even join the paper. Junior is scary.

Shane shows me the story he wrote about a school evacuation drill. I'll never tell him, but I think his story's pretty good. I particularly like the way he finishes by saying that even though we were all out in the parking lot, to protect us from some kind of bomb explosion, if there had been a bomb, we all would have been hit by flying building parts anyway.

Shane's asking me what I wrote about, but I won't tell him. What's a cockroach compared to a bomb?

Although, my brother Jack once told me that if a nuclear bomb destroyed everything on Earth— all the people, the animals, the plants—if that happened, the cockroaches would survive. They'd be the only things left on Earth. So maybe my cockroach story *is* important.

Alyce wrote about the fashion show the sewing classes are planning. Alyce is interested in clothes. I didn't tell her, either.

When Mr. Fischer walks in, he's holding our stories.

"I got a number of submissions," he says. "And I've printed out some of them, without the names, so that we can discuss them in detail."

Don't let my story be one of them. Please don't let it be mine.

The first story Mr. Fischer reads isn't mine; it's Shane's. Afterward, Mr. Fischer talks about how Shane has all the important elements in his first paragraph—Mr. Fischer calls it the lead. I write down that word. But then he asks the kids what they think of the statement: "Students might not be safe in the parking lot, where they could still be harmed by the explosion."

All the kids are saying that that was a really good thing to put in, because if there really were a bomb, kids could get badly injured. Someone says that the building could fall on us. Mr. Fischer doesn't seem to agree. He's shaking his head. Does he think the building wouldn't fall? Was that wrong?

"Actually, what this writer has done is to insert his own opinion into the story. News reports are concerned only with the facts. Opinions belong in editorials. Now, I'm not saying that this reporter didn't make a good point. He did. But what should he have done, if he questioned the safety of the evacuation?"

Everyone's looking blank. Even Shane. I wish I knew the right answer so I could raise my hand and tell Mr. Fischer.

"What he should have done," Mr. Fischer says, "was talk to the person in charge of security for the school, ask that person if he thought students standing in the parking lot might be injured by the explosion. Then the reporter would have a response to put into his story. The reporter asks questions and reports the answers. Readers will draw their own conclusions."

I get what Mr. Fischer is saying, but most of the kids are still looking confused.

"Let me hand out another story and see what you think of this one."

Oh no, it's my story. Or maybe my obituary. My hands are sweating so badly, the ink is coming off on my fingers. I won't raise my hand again this afternoon.

When the other kids read the story, they start to laugh—the faster readers laugh first, but after a while, everybody's had a turn. I want to cry, but I pretend to laugh along with everyone else. So they won't know I wrote it.

"Okay, people, settle down."

Mr. Fischer is smiling, a big grin. He knows who wrote the stupid story; he'd never say my name to the group, but he knows it was me. I can't ever face him again. Do eleven-year-old girls ever have sudden heart attacks? I think I'm feeling a very sharp pain in my left side.

"Does this reporter cover essential elements in the lead?"

A chorus of yeses. At least they've stopped laughing.

"But I want to point out something that this reporter has done. She's—"

Why did he have to say "she"? That narrows down the possible suspects.

"She's followed up on her story with a number of interviews. And she concludes with a statement by the janitor that really wraps up the whole thing. It's always a good idea to try to get statements from the people involved in your story. And use direct quotations when you can. In other words, when you're interviewing people, if they say something you think is interesting, write down exactly what they said. Quoting other people in your article keeps your readers interested. And I have to say, this writer used some striking quotations."

Hold on—don't remove the body just yet. I think I detect some signs of life.

"One other thing—" Mr. Fischer is saying, and he's looking pleased. "A piece of journalistic ethics. The teacher asked that his name not be used, and the reporter respected that request. You must always make sure, before you quote someone, that you have his or her permission. However . . ."

Uh-oh.

"However, I should point out a couple of areas that an editor would correct—a matter of word choices. Look at the last sentence in the first paragraph. Anyone want to play editor here?"

Shane raises his hand. Of course.

"I'm not sure she should have called the cockroach an 'invading culprit.' The writing seems a little, I don't know, dramatic."

Shane is smirking. He knows it was me who wrote it. I'd give him my death stare, but then he'd know for sure that I wrote the cockroach story.

"You're right," Mr. Fischer says.

Shane turns to look at me, probably to gloat. But I keep my eyes straight ahead, and my face very serious, as though the story was somebody else's.

"Those words," Mr. Fischer goes on, "are making a judgment about the cockroach. News reports must be neutral. Anything else?"

Oh no, not Shane again.

"I'm not sure about the last sentence, where she says 'unfortunate' incident. Maybe just 'incident' would have been enough."

Okay, if Shane wants to play his silly little games with me, let him. By now he's probably convinced Mr. Fischer that my story's no good—too "dramatic," Shane called it.

"I have to agree about those two little word choices, but all in all, I'd have to say this was a first-rate piece of reporting."

First rate. I'm still trying to look serious, but I'm breathing really fast. And I'm feeling so hot I bet my face is all red. *First rate.* I don't care if Shane laughs until his head explodes, Mr. Fischer said my article was first rate.

Callie's Rules: What I Know About Boys:

- Boys like to win.
- Girls like to win, too, but we don't gloat.

Mr. Fischer hands out some other stories for us to discuss, but I hardly even look at them. I'm looking at Mr. Fischer. Someday, I know, he's going to be reading stories written by C. X. Jones. And I'll come back here and I'll find him and I'll say, "Mr. Fischer, do you remember me? I got my start right here, on *The Hawk*."

Mr. Fischer will look exactly the same as he does now, but I won't. I won't be a kid. I'll be beautiful.

3 Keeping Up at the Joneses

If I'm going to be a reporter, it's not too soon to start thinking like a reporter. So here's how I'd write my next story.

> *On Tuesday night, eight members of the Jones family gathered around the dinner table to discuss the events of each person's day, the most important being the selection of one of the daughters to be a reporter on the newly formed middle-school newspaper,* The Hawk.

Boy, that has got to be the longest sentence ever written, but I needed to get all the important facts into the lead. This newspaper reporting is going to be harder than I thought.

Present were Herman Jones, the father; Mary Jones, the mother; Andromeda, known as Andy, at fifteen the oldest girl; Calliope (Callie), eleven, the budding reporter; Melpomene (Mel), ten; twin boys, Ted and Fred, seven; and Polyhymnia (Polly), four. The oldest son, Jack, who is seventeen, is away at a debate tournament.

Boy, is this story ever boring. But that's okay; our family story wouldn't ever be in a newspaper. More likely in *Mad* magazine. (My brother Jack, the one who's away, used to let me read his copies.) We're all so different, sometimes it's hard to believe we're related. Take my parents, for example. They're married, but they couldn't be more different from each other. My father is a lawyer. My lead said that the family was going to discuss each person's day, but my father never does. He says it would be "unethical" for him to talk about his cases. Then there's my mother. She's a metal sculptor. She doesn't ever talk about her work, either; she just shows it to us. Some of her work is really beautiful, but not too many people get it—a lot of them look confused and then they ask her what her sculptures are supposed to be.

Even we kids are all different, except for the twins, who look alike. But I don't want to talk about the other kids right now. The really important thing, the thing any reader would want to know, is about my being chosen for the newspaper. I'm all set to start telling about it, but Polly insists she has to tell first—or rather sing first. She's just started preschool and she thinks she's the first person to ever learn the song "Little Ducky Duddle." (All of us kids sang it, and we sure don't want to hear it again.)

> *"Little Ducky Duddle*
> *Went swimming in a puddle,*
> *Went swimming in a puddle quite small."*

This is definitely not a song that's ever going to appear on anybody's playlist—anybody past kindergarten, that is. But that doesn't seem to bother Polly. She's still singing.

"Said she, it doesn't matter,
How much I splash and splatter.
I'm only a ducky after all."

She's about to repeat the whole silly song from the beginning when my mother jumps in (into Polly's song, not the puddle). "That was lovely, Polyhymnia. Just lovely. Who else has something to tell us?"

My turn.

"I'm going to be a reporter for the school newspaper. They even chose my name for the paper. And Mr. Fischer said my story was a first-rate piece of reporting—"

"Hold on a minute, Callie," my father interrupts. "This is big news. Why don't you slow down and start from the beginning. What name did you suggest? Who is this Mr. Fischer? And tell us about your story."

"Mr. Fischer?" Andy burbles. "Oh, I remember him. He was so cute. I kept wishing all year that I'd had him for English. Instead of old Pelican-Face Pelham. Mr. Fischer was just adorable."

I'd better stop Andy pretty quick, or else she'll

go on and on about Mr. Fischer and I'll never be able to tell about me. Andy monopolizes every conversation.

I go back to the beginning—how the paper's just getting started and how everyone voted for the name I thought of, *The Hawk*. And then I start to tell them about my first story. I've just said that a cockroach crawled out of Sophia Meyer's gym shorts, when Andy shrieks.

"Eeew! Caaal-*lie*! That's so disgusting. Now I won't be able to eat another bite."

"Shut up, Andy! If you're so sensitive, don't listen."

Callie's Rule:

- If you want to gross out your teenage sister, talk about cockroaches while she's eating.

"Andromeda. Calliope." That's my mother. She's the only person who calls us by our actual, ridiculous names. "Keep that up and you'll both have to leave the table. Now go on, Calliope. No, wait. First apologize to your sister."

So I do. Apologize. Actually, I say "sorry" so quietly

that Andy practically has to read my lips. Then I run up to my room and get my story to read to them. So they'll get to hear the good writing.

All the time I'm reading it, the twins are poking each other with their elbows and practically rolling out of their seats, laughing. I ignore them.

Callie's Rule:

• Boys are never grossed out by cockroaches. It's a gene thing.

When I've finished, I tell them about how Mr. Fischer liked my doing the interviews and using quotations.

"Shane's going to be on the paper. Alyce is, too. Shane did a really good story on this thing that they make us do, where there's supposed to be an emergency in the school, like a bomb or something, although there really isn't, and we all have to 'evacuate' the school and stand in the parking lot.

"Everybody thinks those drills are pretty stupid, and there has never been a real bomb. I wouldn't have thought of doing a story about them. But at the end of the story, Shane said he thought it wasn't safe to have the kids out in the parking lot because if there really were an explosion, the kids could get hurt from pieces of the building falling on them or the windows blowing out.

"I thought that was a really good idea, but Mr. Fischer said Shane shouldn't have put his opinion into a news report. Mr. Fischer said Shane should have gone to the person in charge and asked him about it."

"Mr. Fischer was right. It's the same as in a court of law." That, of course, is my father. "A lawyer never injects his own opinions; he asks the questions that will give him the answer he wants."

"What story are you going to do next, Callie?" Mel asks.

"Oh, Mel. I don't know. I've been keeping my eyes peeled, just like Mr. Fischer told us to do, but I haven't seen anything I can write about."

"Maybe," my father says, with a little smile, "you ought to keep in mind what *Mr. Fischer*—"

Why did my father put so much stress on Mr. Fischer's name when he said it? And why is he smiling? He's getting at something—I know he is. That's what my father does. He never tells us what to do; he says he wants us to think and find the answers for ourselves. Okay, so I'm thinking. And not finding anything.

And then, the tiniest thing does pop into my head.

"Questions," I say. "Mr. Fischer wants us to ask questions."

"Right," my father says. "What kind of questions?"

"Shane needs to go to whoever's in charge of those drills and interview him. Ask him about whether it would be safe for everyone to be standing outside if there really were a bomb."

"But Callie," Mel bursts in, "Shane's already got a story. What about you? You need one."

"Right. I do, but . . ." I'd had another tiny thing in my head, but when Mel started talking, I lost it. What was it? What was I thinking before?

"Interviews. I'm good at interviews." That's it. "Shane and I can do this story together. We can go and talk to whoever's in charge and get his answer. Shane had the idea, but I'm good at interviews. I'd better call Shane right away and tell him. Before he decides to do the interviews all by himself."

4 Chief Bloodworth

I had no idea that security was such a big deal. The town actually has someone in charge of it, someone by the name of Chief Bloodworth, Chief of Security Bloodworth. Shane and I had to make an appointment just to talk to him. And now we're sitting and waiting for him in his office. His secretary said he's in a very important meeting that might run a bit long, but that he's looking forward to talking with us.

I feel as though we're sitting in a stainless-steel refrigerator. Everything in the room is square and gray and shiny. The walls are gray; the linoleum squares on the floor are gray. The desk and the file cabinets are gray. Even the chairs are gray metal. (And very hard to sit on.) Behind the desk are two flags—one U.S. and one New Jersey—and their bright colors against the square gray walls make me think of the blueberries and strawberries my mother freezes in ice cubes for summer drinks. Between the flags is a large picture of the president, in shades of gray. Facing us, on the front of the desk, is a metal nameplate with CHIEF BLOODWORTH in black letters. On one side of the desk are three law books. (I know they're law books because they're all boring brown, like the ones in my father's office.) On the other side are six sharpened pencils, all exactly the same height, standing in a straight row in a metal holder.

We've been sitting for a very long time, and my bottom is going numb. (I wish I didn't have such a skinny butt.) Shane and I don't say a word. Maybe we've been sitting in this fridge so long our vocal cords have frozen.

Finally, Chief Bloodworth marches in. Something about him makes Shane and me jump to our feet. Maybe it's his uniform. Or maybe we just can't sit in those chairs another minute.

"At ease, soldiers. No need to stand at attention." Chief Bloodworth laughs, but his mouth doesn't move. "Sit down. You must be the students from the school. I'm Chief Bloodworth, but you can call me Chief."

Chief's hair is gray and cut so short you can see his pink scalp through it. It's hard to see his eyes; he looks as though he's squinting, like he's spent too many years in the sun without sunglasses.

"I'm glad you came to see me today. Excellent, excellent. Newspapers are the most effective way for us to get our message out. And school newspapers are the best way to get our message out to you kids."

I wish he hadn't called us kids; it would have been better if he'd called us reporters, the way Mr. Fischer did.

"I understand you have a question for me."

Shane doesn't even open his mouth. He's probably still frozen, so I guess I'd better do the asking. Either that or we'll both sit here looking like people in a natural history museum.

"Yes, sir," I say. "I had a question about the security drill at the middle school." I get ready to write down Chief's answer in my notebook. "I know we're supposed to line up in the parking lot—just as if there is a real bomb, or whatever—

so we won't get hurt. But if there *is* a real bomb, and the building explodes, isn't it just as dangerous to be standing right outside? In the parking lot?"

I can feel Shane glaring at me. I know this was his idea, but he didn't ask the question, so I had to.

Chief is smiling now. "Okay, good question. All the kids are leaving the building and going into the parking lot?"

We nod.

"And you're waiting there until you get the all-clear signal?"

We nod again.

"Good. That's what you're supposed to do. Anything else you'd like to ask me? That's what I'm here for, to answer your questions. And I think there's a very important question you should be asking right now. You should be asking me why we have those security drills in the first place. Well, let me tell you that we have those drills to protect you—to protect you from terrorism. America, the country where you were born, the country that has given you the prosperity and freedom that you enjoy, the America you love, is being threatened by a terrible menace—the menace of terrorism."

Chief looks hard, first at Shane, then at me. It's scary when someone stares at you, even scarier when you can't see their eyes. I feel better when Chief turns away and looks back at the American flag behind him.

"I know you've heard about the terrorist threat, but here's something you may not know—these people are right here in our very own country. They may even be living, and carrying out their sinister mission, in our own town of Hillcrest, even now plotting to destroy us. I think you'll want to write about this for your newspaper."

I don't think this is something we can put in *The Hawk.* Mr. Fischer said we had to write about school news. I open my mouth to ask Chief about the security drill, but he goes right on talking.

"And do you know," Chief bellows, pointing a finger at us, "who those people are who hate our democratic way of life, our tolerance and mutual respect?"

Shane practically bursts from his chair. "The skinheads?"

I thought that was a really good answer, but Chief looks confused.

"No, no, no. It's the terrorist network. The terrorist network is like a giant octopus, and it's stretching its ugly tentacles everywhere, each of those tentacles shooting out its dark poison of intolerance, destruction, and death."

I always thought octopus ink came from their heads, but maybe I wasn't paying attention that day in science.

"We have to defend ourselves. I can see from your faces that you two are pretty worried. And, well, you should be. But as President Truman once said, 'Education is our first line of defense.' And that's why you two are so important. You can go back to your newspaper and educate your fellow students about the terrorist threat.

"So I guess I've pretty much covered it," Chief says. "Is there anything else you'd like to ask me?"

Shane's mouth is open, but he doesn't say a word. He looks like he's frozen—must be the room. Or maybe he's afraid he'll say the wrong thing, like when he answered that it was the skinheads. Looks like it's up to me.

"Chief . . ." I feel as though my vocal cords have frozen, too. "Chief, I have another question about those security drills. Sometimes kids will call in about a fake bomb—you know, to get out of a test or something. Or even just for a joke. So I don't see—"

"That's breaking the law—a pretty serious offense. And kids who do that are just abetting the terrorists. They'd better be careful. One of these days it might be a real attack, not just a drill, and then . . . I think I ought to talk to your principal, Mr. Nolan, about that. We can't let these kinds of dangerous acts continue."

Oh no. He's going to talk to Mr. No-Man. Chief will say that I was the one who told him, and for sure I'll be in serious trouble. Even though I haven't done anything wrong. That's just the way it is. That's the way it was last year, when I was standing at the bus line asking kids to sign my petition to save Halloween. And he said I was "disrupting the bus lines" and "defying authority." Well, I guess I was defying authority. In a way. But I thought that asking people to sign a petition was allowed in a democracy. No, middle school's no democracy. Not when Mr. No-Man's the principal. I can't let Chief talk to him. I've got to stop him. Right now.

"Chief," I blurt, not having any idea what I'm going to say next. And then, of course, I don't say anything.

"Chief," Shane cuts in, "we know you're pretty busy here, watching out for terrorists and all, so Callie and I could talk to Mr. Nolan about the fake bomb scares."

Saved! Tough as it will be, I'll have to thank Shane later.

"Okay," Chief says. "Why don't you kids do that? It's good that you two want to show some public spiritedness."

Chief walks around to the front of his desk. Funny, when he walked in, he seemed so big, but he isn't. He has a big body, but he's really kind of short and wide, with short legs. He puts a hand on each of our shoulders and smiles at us.

"Look, kids, I know you're pretty scared about the terrorists. And doing the right thing in an emergency will help a lot. But let me tell you, the terrorists can do a lot worse than just blowing up your school. I'll tell you what I think. I don't think the terrorists are going to bomb us. That's not the real threat. I think they're going to release chemicals into our water systems, into the air. And that's why I'm asking the school district to hand out metal dog tags to the students. Can you think why?"

We shake our heads.

"Because in case of a chemical air attack, those tags'll be the only way to identify the bodies."

Chief's still smiling. How can he smile? Doesn't he know what he just said? Can't he see those melted faces? I can. And I feel like screaming.

Callie's Rule:

- The people who are supposed to be keeping us safe can be as scary as the terrorists.

"So you see," he says, "we have got to defeat those terrorists, destroy them before they destroy us. Any other questions?"

Neither of us can say a word. Shane's turned white. My knees are shaking so badly I have to hold on to the arms of the chair as I get up.

"Th-Thank you," is all I can manage.

"Just remember what I told you. And keep on

the lookout for those terrorists. They could be any-where—in your town, in your neighborhood, even in your school. So keep your eyes and your ears open. And if you see or hear anything suspicious, tell someone right away."

5 Sandwiches and a Story

Shane and I are sitting at the kitchen table. He's already eaten three sandwiches—Shane says if he's hungry, his brain shuts down—but we're running out of peanut butter.

Finally, he pushes his plate aside and says, "Okay, Cal, I'm ready to start writing."

"Fine, Shane, but while you were busy cleaning out our kitchen, I already got half the story written. We'll put this part after your story about the school security drill."

"Let me see." Shane grabs the pad I'd been writing on. I'm not allowed to use Jack's laptop without his permission. Shane starts to read, then his face scrunches up in a frown.

"What's the matter, Shane? Is my story 'too dramatic'?"

"I have no idea. I can't read your writing at all."

"Here." I snatch the pad back from him. "I'll read it to you.

"Chief Bloodworth is the head of homeland security for the entire town of Hillcrest—"

Shane interrupts me. "You can't start like that, Cal."

"Why not, Shane? There's not one thing wrong with that entire sentence."

"Yes, there is. You have to give Chief's whole name."

"I did."

"You didn't. You didn't say his first name."

"We don't know his first name."

"Well, we've got to put it in. At least the first time. After that we can just use his last name. Good thing I had something to eat, kept my brain working. Maybe you should eat something, Cal."

"Shane, if you're going to be like that, you can just go home right now."

"Sorry."

Shane doesn't often say "sorry." It must have been the threat of cutting off his food supply.

"But really, Cal, we don't know Chief's first name."

"Hand me the phone book, Shane. It's right behind you."

"What are you going to do? Call him up and ask him? That'll go over big."

I don't bother to answer. But in a few seconds I have what I'm looking for.

"Hapworth," I say. "Chief's name is Hapworth Bloodworth."

"No, it's not. You're kidding, Cal."

"I'm not kidding. You were ragging on me, but I found it right here, under Bloodworth. Not Chief. I've heard that starvation sharpens your mental powers. You ought to try it sometime, Shane."

I shove the phone book toward Shane.

"Maybe his mother," I say, "was on some kind of painkiller when she named him. But anyway, his real name is Hapworth Bloodworth. I wonder if his wife calls him Chief."

"She sure wouldn't call him Happy," Shane says.

Shane starts looking around like he wants to make another sandwich.

"Shane! There isn't any more peanut butter."

"Okay, then, read me the rest of what you've got."

"*Recently, Chief Bloodworth spoke to two reporters from* The Hawk. *Chief Bloodworth feels that it is very important to get his message out to students.*

"He said 'kids,' Shane, but I thought students sounded better.

"*The message that the Chief wanted to give to students is that*—

"This is a direct quote, Shane.

"*—is that America 'is being threatened by a terrible menace—the menace of terrorism.' He went on to say that there may be terrorists even in our town of Hillcrest. He said that those terrorists might pretend to be ordinary people, but that 'they're plotting to destroy us.'*

"That was another quote, Shane."

"Okay, Cal, I get it. Go on."

"That's all I've got so far. Chief didn't say too much that we could use in our article."

"You forgot where you asked him about kids calling in a fake bomb. We should put that in—it's really important. Here, I'll write that part."

I hand Shane the pad and pencil. He looks through his own notes from the interview and starts writing.

"Chief Bloodworth said that when kids call in a fake bomb threat, they're breaking the law. He said that it not only is a serious offense but that kids who do that are 'abetting the terrorists.'"

"Good for you, Shane. You used a quotation."

Shane glares at me.

"Wait a sec, Shane. I've got a brilliant conclusion. I'll just write it and you can tell me what you think.

"Homeland Security Chief Bloodworth had one more important point he wanted to make. He's asking the school district to hand out metal dog tags to the students . . . because in case of a chemical air attack, 'those tags'll be the only way to identify the bodies.'"

"Wow!" That's all Shane can manage to say. Just "wow!" I know how he feels.

And now when I reread Shane's part of the story, it all seems kind of plain compared to what I wrote.

"Hold on, Shane, I want to add some stuff."

Shane is looking hungry again, but I ignore him. I've got to concentrate.

"Okay, Shane, you can read it now."

Shane snatches the story from me, reads it, then sneers at me. "You can't put that in, Callie."

"Can't put what in?"

"The stuff you just added. Like here, where you say, 'throngs of students hastened from their classrooms and into the parking lot.' Or here, 'for some moments confusion and disorder were rampant.' I mean, Cal, you're really getting carried away."

"I am not. That's good writing, Shane; it's exciting. What you wrote was just a dull report."

"That's what a news story is—a report."

"But not a dull one!"

"Or what about here, where you say, 'several students expressed vociferous objections to having to stand for a protracted period in the hot sun.' Geez, Cal, you might as well be writing a vocabulary test. What you put in is just—"

"Just what? Too dramatic?"

"Yeah, it is."

"Fine. So take out what I wrote and just hand in your boring old article." I snatch the plate away from Shane just as he's about to put out his finger to pick up the remaining crumbs.

"Don't get mad, Callie. Just 'cause I wanted to take out what you wrote . . ."

"I'm not mad. I just think we're finished. The article is the way you want it, so that's fine."

I slam Shane's plate into the sink. Good thing I gave him a plastic plate.

"You can go home now, Shane. The article's done, and there's nothing left to eat."

Two More Rules About Writing:

- Never eat before writing. Writers do their best work when they're hungry— like starving artists.
- Food clogs the brain passages, making the writing boring.

6 All Sewn Up

Let Shane have the stupid article his way. I'm going to write something much better, something that will remain in the annals of Hillcrest Middle School as the most brilliant story ever to appear in *The Hawk*. Or I will write it once I come up with a good idea. But right now I have nothing.

In school, my eyes are everywhere, my ears are everywhere, but there's nothing.

"Are you wearing jeans or a dress to the dance Friday night?"

"I hate science class. Who cares about pea plants. Who knew that peas have parents?"

"Well, I'm not a pea, but my parents will kill me if I don't get good grades this semester."

"You'll never guess what happened to Chiara."

I never do find out what happened to Chiara. That might have been something worth writing about. But I have nothing. *Nothing*.

And then suddenly there is something. The worst something possible. Alyce and I are walking out of social studies class, when Shane passes us, turns around, and smirks at me. "Have you got another story yet, Cal?"

"Yes, I have. Alyce and I are going to write about the sewing classes' fashion show."

I don't know where that came from—I have this way of just blurting things out before I think—but it's out now, and I'm stuck with it. Shane's trying not to laugh, and Alyce is bouncing like a Ping-Pong ball, she's so happy. I'm the only one who's not.

"Callie, you'll do the story with me? That's great. You're a much better writer than me. It'll be so much fun."

Fun! Right. I won't have sewing again until next year. But last fall's sewing class was one of the most ghastly experiences I've ever had in my life, so ghastly that even now when I think about it, my stomach crawls up into my chest and my brain wants to duck down and join it.

It just seems so unfair that we have to suffer this way. Sewing classes are so nineteenth century. We must be the only school in the entire state, the entire country, the entire developed world, where the girls are still required to take sewing. And it's all because of Miss Stern. She's the sewing teacher, and she's very old. Very, very old. And that's the reason we all have to take sewing. Miss Stern started teaching sewing a long, long time ago. After a while, they wanted to eliminate sewing as a requirement, but Miss Stern was still not old enough to retire and get a pension, and there was nothing else she was qualified to teach, so they let her keep on teaching sewing. And making all of us girls suffer through it.

The sixth-grade sewing class always has to make skirts. Last fall, when I had sewing, Miss Stern chose a pattern for a full skirt with a contrasting band of fabric at the hem. It was supposed to be for spring. I went with my mother to the fabric store to get what I needed. That's where the nightmare began. My mother picked out a dark green cotton for the skirt and a rust cotton for the hem. Lovely. Except that in class the next day, I saw that everyone else had picked pastels—pink, blue, light green, yellow—with flowers all over and a solid color for the bottom. (After they'd finished their skirts, they were going to cut the hems off the skirts and shorten them.)

So every day, from 10:05 until 10:45, I sat like a giant question mark hunched over that sewing machine. I never looked up. I knew what I'd be seeing if I did: Miss Stern's pinned-together brows and sewed-down mouth. I didn't have to look up to hear her voice, like an unoiled sewing machine, telling me she'd never seen such a clumsy sewing student in all her years of teaching.

You'd think I could make a simple, stupid machine do what I wanted, just sew the seams straight. But I couldn't. Over and over and over again, Miss Stern made me rip out my seams and redo them. The rest of the class had already finished their skirts and taken them home and shortened them, and I hadn't even put the zipper in mine. Which was probably just as well. I was never, ever going to wear that totally wrong skirt.

Callie's Rules About Sewing Teachers:

• Sewing teachers should never be allowed to teach sewing. The school should just keep them around to fix things, like when a button pops off your pants in math class.
• If there were a sewing assistant, you wouldn't have to go to the nurse's office to ask for a safety pin and have everyone staring at it for the rest of the day. Even if they had heard the button pop off and roll down the aisle and they'd stared at you then.

Shane's voice breaks into my nightmare.

"Well, okay, then, Cal. You go do that fashion show story with Alyce. I've got to give the school security article to Mr. Fischer."

Mr. Fischer. Shane's going to see Mr. Fischer. And tell him that the story is all his own. And get credit for the whole thing. I wrote a lot of that story. Even if Shane did take out my best parts. This is so not fair. Not even by Shane's rules. Well,

I have my own rules, and I feel one coming on right now.

Callie's Rule:

- Boys should have to take sewing the same as girls. And write about fashion shows, too. Then they wouldn't be so stuck up about school security stories.

"Wait up, Shane. I worked on that story. And the quote I put in from Chief is the best part. I'm going with you."

"Callie? I thought you were going to help *me*."

"I will, Alyce. I can do both."

As we're walking to Mr. Fischer's room, I'm thinking, This is all Shane's fault. It's because of him that I have to do the fashion show story with Alyce. And Shane took out all the best parts of the story—my best writing. I know Mr. Fischer would have really liked what I wrote.

7 Truth and Lies

Mr. Fischer is reading the article, and he's not showing any reaction. Of course not—Shane took out all my really good writing. But when Mr. Fischer gets to the end—where I put in the quotation about the metal dog tags—he frowns. What's wrong?

"This is a direct quote from Chief Bloodworth? The exact words he used? Did Chief Bloodworth actually say that he's 'asking the school district to hand out metal dog tags to the students . . . because in case of a chemical air attack, those tags'll be the only way to identify the bodies'?"

Oh, that's the problem. Mr. Fischer thought I might have misquoted.

"Those were his exact words, Mr. Fischer. I had a notebook and when Chief said that, I wrote it down exactly the way he said it, the way you told us to. And I made sure to put quotation marks around it so that later I'd know that it was a direct quote."

Mr. Fischer is probably thinking that Callie Jones is going to be the best, most accurate reporter on *The Hawk*.

"I'm sorry, Callie, Shane, but I think we have to take that statement out of the article."

"Why?" I just blurted out that *why*? but I don't want to hear the answer. Right now, the only thing I want is to disappear. Fast. Like that cockroach in the girls' locker room.

"Callie, I have to take out the quotation because it's just too alarming for a school newspaper. Chief Bloodworth is saying that there'll be nothing to identify but metal tags. I think you can see why we can't print that."

"Wow," I say. "That sounds even more disgusting than cockroaches."

Where was that pause button when I needed it? I mean, what I just said was what my mother would call "totally inappropriate." Mr. Fischer doesn't say a word. Maybe he didn't hear what I said. Or maybe he wishes he hadn't. I really wish I hadn't said it. I promise myself I won't say another word.

"Chief said a lot of other things, too," Shane says. "It didn't really have to do with school, though."

"What else did Chief Bloodworth tell you?"

"He told us a lot of stuff about the terrorists. He said they're right here in America. He said they might even be right here in Hillcrest. He said they're getting organized here, planning to commit crimes."

"But, Shane . . ." I know I promised myself I'd keep quiet, but Shane's acting so superior. "But, Shane, when Chief asked if we knew who wanted to do all of that—you know, commit crimes, destroy our way of life, eliminate tolerance and mutual respect—you said it was the skinheads."

That should knock Shane down a foot or two.

"That was actually a good answer, Shane," Mr. Fischer says. "It shows you were thinking for yourself."

Geez, I can't do or say anything right today. Now I've made Shane look good. And made myself look like a complete moron—a motormouthed moron.

"Yeah, I thought it was a good answer. But Chief said he was talking about the terrorists."

"Well, I think we'll just leave that part out of your story. Good job, both of you. When the paper is ready, we'll put this story in. In the meantime, is there anything else you two could be working on?"

"No," Shane mumbles. "Not yet."

At least I have a story. Not a great one—kind of trivial, in fact—but still a story.

"I'll be working with my friend Alyce," I say, "writing about the school fashion show."

"Who knows," Shane bursts out, "maybe a cockroach will crawl out of one of the dresses while the girls are changing. Then you'll have a really good story."

I want to say that I hope it crawls into Shane's shorts, but for once I don't say what I'm thinking. Not in front of Mr. Fischer, anyway.

8 Zippers and Seams

Alyce is waiting to walk me home. Actually, what we do is, she walks me to my house, but when we get there, we're usually not done talking, or really, Alyce isn't done talking, so then she asks me to walk her back to her house. When we reach her house, she offers to walk me halfway home. The movie house is halfway, and we stand in front for a while, reading the coming attractions. Then I say I really have to go home.

Today, before we've even started walking, Alyce bursts out, "Did you ask Mr. Fischer? Can you write about the fashion show with me?"

Alyce bounces a lot. She bounces when she walks, bounces from one foot to the other when she's standing still, bounces in her seat at school. I get tired just looking at her. Today, she's bouncing like a pogo stick.

"What did he say, Callie? Tell me."

"Well, we'll have to write it first before he approves it. But yes, I did tell him I was going to do the fashion show story with you."

Alyce hugs me—hard. She's still bouncing, but I keep myself planted on the sidewalk, and she has to let me go.

"Oh, Callie, it'll be really neat. We'll get to see all the clothes and watch the rehearsals and everything. There's a lot to do, but we've got plenty of time."

"Plenty of time . . . what do you mean?"

"The fashion show's not till May, silly, so we've got nearly four months. First, the girls have to finish all their garments. Then, they have to practice being models—you know, putting one foot in front of the other and walking with a book on their heads. That part's so last century. But you know Miss Stern . . ." Alyce rolls her eyes.

Any other time I would have made some remark about putting one foot in front of the other being the only way you can walk, unless you want to go backward, but something Alyce said before that stopped me. The fashion show's not until May. A lot can happen before then. I might even find a really good story to write, one that Mr. Fischer will like. There's hope for me yet.

"And it's not just the sewing classes that will be working on the show. The music classes will be practicing; the art classes will make posters and programs; the audiovisual kids will work on lighting. The fashion show is pretty important: everything has to be just right.

"And when we write the article, Callie, you can't call what the girls are wearing 'clothes.'"

"Why not? I hope they won't come out in their underwear."

"Don't be silly, Callie. You have to call them 'garments.'"

Alyce is going on about the clothes and all the preparations, and I'm looking straight at her, as though I'm listening, but really I've already got a scene going on in my head.

The spring fashion show, put on by the Hillcrest Middle School sewing classes, was held last night in the school auditorium. There was much anticipation and exhilaration backstage as the girls began dressing in the garments they had designed and executed.

One by one, the models paraded across the stage of the auditorium, proudly displaying their creations. There was a murmur of confusion from the spectators when each of the models glided in balancing a book on her head. The announcer, however, put all confusion to rest when she explained that the books represented the theme of the show, Student Seamstresses.

Alyce has still more important things to tell me. "You have to talk about things like 'extraordinary color sense' and 'fine tailoring.' And all the colors," Alyce is saying, "have to have special names, like 'sea mist' and 'ashes of roses.'"

"Ashes are gray, Alyce, even burnt-rose ashes."

"Don't worry about that, Callie; our readers will understand."

And Shane thought *my* writing was too dramatic. Well, what would Shane think of this scene?

A disaster seemed to loom when Sandy Mulcahey spilled root beer over her "bright-sunrise" blouse. Sandy's extraordinary color sense, however, served her well, when she dabbed her blouse dry and declared that it was now patterned in a color she called antique raisin.

Alyce is getting really excited now. She's practically leaping.

"Now, the sixth-grade girls will wear the skirts they're making. The seventh-graders are making blouses, and the eighth-graders jackets."

"Hold on a minute, Alyce. You just said the sixth-grade girls will wear skirts, the seventh-graders will wear blouses, and the eighth-graders will wear jackets. This show is never gonna happen."

"Why not, Callie? Do you know something?"

"I don't know much about 'garments' or 'fine tailoring,' but I do know that the school will never allow any girl to walk across the stage of the auditorium wearing only a skirt. Or even worse, only a blouse or a jacket."

"You're being mean, Callie, and I'm not sure I want to do this story with you."

Alyce looks like she's going to cry. Sometimes I do that to her—I get sarcastic and hurt her feelings.

"I'm sorry, Alyce. I meant it to be funny, but I guess it wasn't."

All went well, but an emergency arose when the zipper on Caitlin Diaz's skirt jammed and could not be closed. Miss Stern, the sewing teacher, rose to the rescue and snipped open the skirt. On examination of the offending item, the instructress determined that Caitlin had not left a sufficient overlap, and she sent the designer back to the sewing room to renovate her garment. Unfortunately, the operation took over two hours, and Caitlin was not able to appear in the show.

"Is there anything else I should know, Alyce?"
"Oh, there's lots more, but I'll teach it to you."
"Thanks, I appreciate that."

The audience, consisting of families and friends of the models, responded with enormous enthusiasm. It should be noted, however, that after the intermission, many of the fathers remained outside. They did return at the end of the show and applauded the girls' final bows with the utmost vigor.

I've just thought of two more rules.

Callie's Rules About Fashion:

- Fashion rules don't make any sense.
- But you have to act as though they do.

9 Reporting Like a Reporter

It's gonna be in! My story! My one and a half stories, actually!

Okay, Callie, get a grip. Start over and tell it like a reporter. Here goes.

The first issue of *The Hawk,* which is due to be published in two weeks, will include, on the front page, two stories by Callie Jones: one that is entirely her own and one that she wrote in collaboration with Shane Belcher.

All right. Now I can tell the whole story the way I want to.

At the last meeting, when Mr. Fischer handed back some of the stories, he'd written lots of comments in the margins. I don't know what he wrote, but some of the kids didn't look too happy. A couple of them crumpled up their papers. After the meeting, I heard one kid, one of the ones who'd crumpled up his paper, say that he was going to quit the newspaper because baseball practice would be starting soon. Actually, baseball season is at least two months away. And I was thinking that even if I had been the star pitcher, I wouldn't have quit the paper.

Uh-oh. I'm getting off the subject again. Well, after Mr. Fischer handed back the stories, he read a list of the ones he'd decided to include in the first issue. And I had two stories on that list! To tell the truth, it's actually one and a half—my cockroach story and the school security story I wrote with Shane. So the final score is Callie 1.5, Shane .5. But I plan to be a very big person and not gloat.

One person I'm not going to gloat to is Alyce. She's going to have a story in, too. She won't tell me what she wrote—says she's afraid I'll laugh. I say I promise not to laugh, and besides, she's my best friend and don't best friends tell each other everything? So then she tells me. Part of it. All she'll say is that her story is about a hamster. I promised Alyce I wouldn't laugh, so I don't. Even though I want to. But then I remember that my whole story is about a cockroach, so maybe there isn't anything to laugh about.

Mr. Fischer says he has to run the stories by Mr. Nolan, for his approval, but in the meantime, we're to get the paper ready to go to press. When Mr. Fischer said those words—"go to press"—I felt my head get all prickly.

Two weeks! The first issue of *The Hawk* will appear in two weeks.

10 Censored

The most stupendous thing has happened. We have our own newsroom. This is so like a real newspaper. Now we're not working in a classroom, with the day's homework assignment on the board and some teacher's inspiring posters tacked up all over. This room is just for *The Hawk*. The only assignments are news assignments, and the only things tacked up are layouts for the paper.

Mr. Fischer got the room for us. It used to be the classroom for special-needs kids, but a few years ago all those kids got mainstreamed and the room wasn't being used, so the janitors took it over. Then Mr. No-Man found out that the janitors were smoking in there, and he kicked them out and locked it up again. (I guess just this one time, when Mr. No-Man said no, it turned out to be a good thing—for us.) Anyway, Mr. Fischer got us the room, but when we first went in, it really reeked of smoke.

So today, Andrik brought in a can of air freshener, and he's spraying it everywhere, but that starts a whole big fight. Jamie's yelling—well, not yelling, more like declaring with question marks—that spray cans are destroying the ozone, and that spray cans can't be recycled. Elwin is complaining that he has asthma and that if the spray brings on another attack, he'll wind up in the hospital and his parents will sue the school—or maybe just Andrik.

I'm starting to get worried. This is supposed to be my group, but everyone is getting mad. They're arguing, and I'm thinking they might even start to fight. Then Shane jumps in.

"Elwin," Shane says, "I'm gonna be a lawyer someday. If you can wait a few years before you sue, you can be my first case."

We all stop what we're doing and look at Elwin.

"Hey, Andrik," Elwin says, grinning. "Willing to settle out of court?"

"Sure." Andrik fishes around in his backpack

and pulls out a bag of M&M's. "Will you take these?" And he tosses the bag to Elwin.

Andrik puts away his spray can, and we open the windows. Score one for Shane. I guess if he does become a lawyer, he'll be settling most of his cases out of court. (I learned about that from my father.)

When we've cleaned up the room, Mr. Fischer gets us some long tables and a couple of computers—they're sort of old, but they work okay—and we're all set. We need just one more thing—I make a sign for the outside of the door that says THE HAWK'S NEST.

When I first put the sign up, I kind of worry. Maybe the other kids will think the sign isn't cool. I mean, maybe it's too touchy-feely, like a mother bird with all her chicks. Or Mr. Fischer with all his kids. But I'm starting to feel as though we all do belong together . . . in this room . . . as a group. Turns out, though, that the other kids in the group like the sign. Except for Andrik, who says that a nest should be on the roof, not on the ground floor, but that's Andrik—he's always got something to say.

So we're all—everybody—in the Hawk's Nest, and Shane and I are trying to decide—well, arguing, really—about whether the cockroach article should go at the top of the page. We go quiet—everyone does—when the door opens and Mr. No-Man unfurls himself into our newsroom.

Mr. Fischer stands up, and the two of them head to a corner of the room. I can't hear what they're saying, but I can see that Mr. Fischer is angry. Mr. No-Man looks over at all of us, and then he seems to be asking Mr. Fischer a question. Mr. Fischer shakes his head, hard. Mr. No-Man says something, jabbing his finger toward Mr. Fischer, and then he stretches himself out the door.

Mr. Fischer stands for about a minute, his arms folded across his chest. Then he asks me to come out into the hall with him.

Everyone's eyes are on me as I walk out. When he closes the door behind us, I feel like I'm in one of those prison movies, and they've just clanged the cell door shut.

"Callie," Mr. Fischer says, and then he stops.

He's looking angry. Is it something I did? Is Mr. Fischer going to fire me from *The Hawk*? What did I do? Can I fix it?

"Callie, I'm afraid that Mr. Nolan won't let us run your cockroach story. He feels it will reflect badly on the school; he's worried that parents will complain about unhealthy conditions in the locker rooms. I couldn't make him change his mind. Actually, he wanted to tell you himself, but I thought it would be better if I did. I'm really sorry, Callie. Are you okay?"

I'm not okay. I'm not at all okay. I feel all heavy and sore inside, as though my lungs have turned to wet clay. Just the same, I want Mr. Fischer to see that I'm strong, that I can handle this. I'm just about to say "I'm fine," in a brave but casual way, and I open my mouth to speak, but then, up from my wet, heavy chest, comes a gargantuan, grotesque, galumping *hiccup*.

Shame. Humiliation. The ultimate mortification. And Mr. Fischer is smiling. At me.

I want to die. Right here, right now. Fall to the floor in a lifeless lump. Mr. Fischer, don't even bother calling 911. Just let my parents know that their middle daughter has died. A swift but painful death.

"I do that, too, Callie," Mr. Fischer is saying. "When I get upset or nervous, I hiccup. Let's get you a drink of water."

"I'm okay, Mr. Fischer. Really. I'm okay now."

"Well, if you're all right, Callie, I'd better tell the other kids. We'll have to redesign the first page."

I follow Mr. Fischer back into the room. No one's moved since we left; they're all waiting to hear what happened. When Mr. Fischer tells the rest of the kids, they all start grumbling. It turns out they liked my story. They start saying they're really sorry. I thought they'd be mad at me for messing up their paper, but they're really mad at Mr. No-Man. Maybe, just maybe, we are a group. A pretty good group.

And I think that some groups are better than others. Like the girls in the popular group are always cutting one another out. One week one girl gets cut, and the next week she's back and it's a different girl who's out. Or the sports teams—if someone messes up and makes them lose a game, all the others get mad and blame him. But not this group. I don't know, maybe it's because we're *not* popular, *not* big athletic stars, maybe because we know what it's like to be cut out of things . . . I don't know why, but we never do that. We're a pretty good group.

Everyone except for Shane. He doesn't say a word. He's probably gloating.

But the next thing I know, Shane's standing next to me, and he says, "Sorry, Callie. It was a pretty good story." Then he says, "And it was even better after you took out the really dramatic parts." And he grins.

Mr. Fischer isn't saying anything, just sitting at one end of the table with his fist balled up and pressed against his mouth. Then, after a few minutes, he gets up and asks for everyone's attention.

"Sorry to interrupt you," he says, "but I've been doing some thinking. Some people complain when a newspaper prints a story that isn't, well, let's just say a story that makes them uncomfortable, that says something they don't want to read. Mr. Nolan felt that the cockroach article was one of those articles. But a newspaper—a responsible newspaper—has to print those stories even if some readers take offense. And I was thinking that perhaps there are some other things at this school that don't necessarily reflect well on it. So here's a writing exercise I'd like you to try. Of course, this is just an exercise, something to free up your writing muscles. Does anyone have a complaint about something here at Hillcrest Middle School?"

Hands are shooting up like Roman candles on the Fourth of July.

"Mystery meat in the cafeteria on Thursdays."

"That disinfectant they clean the bathrooms with. It makes you want to barf."

"They're repairing the roof above the art room, and the noise is so loud you can't hear the teacher."

"And what about last summer, when the janitors waxed all the floors, and then they put all the furniture back before the wax was dry and all the chairs were stuck to the floor."

"Making everybody wait outside in the winter until the first bell rings. Kids can get really sick."

"Not just in the winter. How about when it's raining really hard?"

I have a complaint—it's about bullies like Junior—but I think for once it would be better if I didn't say what I'm thinking. Elwin's a pretty good kid. I really don't want to embarrass him.

"Okay!" Mr. Fischer practically has to shout over all the kids calling out their complaints. "I can see there's no lack of ideas in this room, so why don't each of you write up your complaint as a letter to the editor. Maybe we'll run some of them."

Mr. Fischer smiles a little half smile.

Then he says, "Mr. Nolan didn't like the cockroach story, but let's see what he thinks of these letters."

Mr. Fischer said that really softly, to himself. I don't think anyone was supposed to hear, but I was sitting right in front of him, and I did.

Everyone gets busy writing. Everyone but me. For once in my life, I can't think of anything to write. And then I do think of something, something for a letter, but not for *The Hawk*. I write:

Dear Shane,
    Thanks for not ragging on me. I know it was hard for you.
    And I should have said it before, but

I didn't. So I'm saying it now. Thank you.

Saying thank you to you was hard for me, too.

Your friend,
Callie

Callie's Rule:

- Sometimes boys can be human. Well, almost human. Sometimes.

11 Writers and Readers

The first issue of *The Hawk* is being published today. (I love that word—*published*.)

Callie Jones published her first article when she was only eleven years old.

We've put bins by the cafeteria, because everybody goes there, with the title of the paper in big letters on the front of the bins. The printer said to expect the copies around ten thirty. Some of the kids have lunch then, so they're going to pick up the papers and distribute them to the boxes. I have third lunch. Third lunch! Five interminable, excruciating, unrelenting periods until lunch.

And then it's there. In the bin just inside the cafeteria door.

Act cool, Callie. Just pick up a copy—okay, a stack of copies—but don't look at the paper yet, just tuck it under your arm and keep walking to your table. Wait until you've unwrapped your sandwich (good thing you're not buying today, waiting in line would take an eternity), then open up a copy and set it down next to you as though you're going to read it while you're eating.

There it is, right in the middle of the front page, the headline "School Emergency Drill," and underneath that, my name. Well, anyway, my name after Shane Belcher's. Shane says it's because he wrote the article first. I say it's alphabetical order. Anyway, there it is: *By Shane Belcher and Callie Jones.* I decided to keep that name for now. That's the name everyone knows me by. When I'm out of school, I'll certainly change it.

Okay, so the story's there. It didn't get accidentally dropped or anything. Don't read it now, Callie. That would definitely not be cool. Just put all the papers into your backpack—careful— don't wrinkle them—and take them home to read later.

Now that I've safely stowed my copies of the paper, I glance around the lunchroom, just casually, to see if anyone else is reading my story. No one nearby is. So I turn back toward the door (where the newspaper bin just happens to be) as though I'm looking for Alyce, who, for some reason, is very late today. No Alyce yet, but kids are picking up the paper as they walk in. But nobody's reading the paper. Why aren't they reading it? It's not as though they're reading their text messages—they're not allowed to have phones in school. That is supposed to keep kids focused. So why aren't they focusing on my article?

Okay, here comes Alyce. I half stand so she'll see me. She does, but she doesn't see the newspaper bin, just walks right by it.

"Callie, are they in? Our stories? Are they in the paper today?"

Our stories . . . I'd forgotten that Alyce had one in, too.

"Geez, Alyce, you walked right by the bin. Why didn't you pick one up?"

"Sorry, Callie. I'll go back and get one."

"Never mind. I've got extras. Take one of mine."

I hand Alyce a paper and watch her while she reads. She reads her story first. Then mine. Alyce is a very slow reader. Ordinarily, that would irritate me, but not today. The longer she takes to read my story, the more people who'll see her reading it. Finally, she's done.

"Callie, that's terrible."

"What's terrible, Alyce? My story?" If Alyce does mean that my story is terrible, I'll never speak to her again until the day I die. And if I die before she does, I'll leave instructions that she is not to come to my funeral.

"No, silly, not your story. The part about how kids who call in fake bomb scares are helping the terrorists. I never thought of that."

"Shane wrote that part."

"Oh. Well, I think the whole article is really good. What did you think of my story?"

Oh no, I hadn't read Alyce's story. I hadn't read anyone's story but mine.

"I really liked it, Alyce. I liked it so much I want to read it again."

So I read Alyce's story—not again, for the first time—and it surprises me. Alyce's story is about a hamster that the science classes were studying. Alyce wrote about that hamster as if it had been a pet that she'd had for years, not just for a few weeks for one period a day. When I get to the part where the hamster dies, for a minute my eyes tear up, and I can't read the end.

When Alyce had told me she was writing about a hamster, I thought that was kind of childish, like something you'd write in third grade. I was wrong. Alyce's writing isn't what Shane would call "dramatic"—just simple words and short sentences. But her story makes me cry.

"Callie," Alyce says after we've talked about her story, "read Elwin's. It's right next to mine."

Elwin's written about a seventh-grade boy who's never been to school before. Well, not a school with other kids in it. The boy was homeschooled until this year, when he persuaded his parents to let him go to school with other kids. Elwin's story is amazing, not at all like Alyce's. Elwin used a lot of the boy's own words—it's hard to quote a hamster—and when I finish reading it, I feel as though I really know the boy, really understand how he feels.

And there's one sentence that I keep going back to, where the kid says, "I wanted to go to a real school because I wanted to be like everyone else.

But now . . . I'm not so sure." I don't know exactly what the kid meant when he said that. Did he mean that he's not like everybody else? Or did he mean that he's not sure he *wants* to be like everybody else? Sometimes I feel that way, like maybe it's okay that I'm different. And what's really strange, when I read that sentence, I keep feeling as if Elwin might feel that way, too.

By the afternoon, some kids have read my article. A few of them tell me that they "liked it." That's all they say, they "liked it." Makes me think of English class, when the teacher asks what a kid thought about a story, and the kids says, "I liked it." If the teacher says, "What did you like about it?" the kid just slumps down in his seat and mumbles, "I don't know, I just liked it."

So I know not to ask anyone what they liked about my article. I'm a kid and much more cool than an English teacher. Except Mr. Fischer, of course.

But I can't stop thinking about Elwin's and Alyce's articles trying to figure out why I like them so much. I mean, they didn't write about anything really important—not like terrorists, or even the school being possibly infested by filthy insects. Alyce wrote about a dead hamster and Elwin about a new boy in school. But both their stories stuck with me. Why?

That night, when I'm squawking at Mel to keep her mess out of my side of the room, it slowly creeps into my head why their stories are so good. Alyce and Elwin weren't worrying about whether their stories would be important. Alyce really cared about the hamster, Elwin really cared about the new boy. And that made me care, too.

Callie's Rule for Writing Stories:

- Important stories aren't always about big subjects. Small things can be important, too, if you care about them in a big way.

12 A Mouse and a Rat

The next morning, as I'm heading to science class, I spot Elwin down the hall. I'm trying to catch up to him, to tell him how good his story is, when I see Junior, the turkey balloon, lumber over to Elwin and shove him against the wall—hard.

I have to swallow down a scream, but Elwin doesn't let on that anything's happened. He doesn't even rub his shoulder, although he must be seriously hurting.

"Oh, sorry," Junior says. "I didn't see you. It's hard to see a little mouse. Good thing I didn't step on you."

The two guys with Junior seem to think he's said something hilarious. Elwin just bends down to pick up his backpack, which had fallen when he got shoved. Then he straightens up and, without even looking at Junior, walks away.

I let him go. Somehow I feel that he'd rather no one had seen what just happened. I wish I hadn't seen it. But I did, and all day the picture of Junior shoving Elwin sloshes around inside me. And there's something else. I keep wondering if I should have done something. But what? As hard as I try, I can't think what I could have done.

As we're leaving school, Alyce is all bubbly about something.

"Callie, I don't think you've heard a word I've been saying."

"Sorry, Alyce. It's just . . . just that I'm not feeling too great right now. I think I'd better go home."

There's only one person whose voice I want to be hearing right now and it's not Alyce. I'm thinking that the one person I want to be hearing is my mother. And I don't think that very often!

I head back to the shed behind our house. That's where my mother does her work, where I'm sure she'll be for the next hour until the younger kids get home from school. All of us kids like to hang out back here. The place is like a museum of Jones Family History. Lined up along the back wall are the eighteen weirdos my mother has made—one each year for Halloween. The weirdos are metal sculptures, in all shapes and sizes, some snarling, some grinning. Just before the holiday, we all carry the weirdos out to the yard and set them up. Some of the weirdos will have lights glowing from their eyes and noses and mouths; one will blow smoke from its ears; another's teeth will rattle when the wind blows. But right now, they're all standing as still and silent as suits of armor.

There's one more weirdo—the best one of all, and the newest—a glorious dragon with shimmering scales and glowing red eyes. The dragon is too big to keep in the shed, so he's been left in the yard, covered with a tarp to protect him from the rain and snow.

My mother sees right away that something's bothering me—she's pretty sharp that way—and she motions me to come sit next to her on a couple of lawn chairs in the back.

"What's wrong, Calliope? Did something happen at school today?"

"Yeah, something did. But not to me. I'm okay. It was Elwin."

"Elwin?"

"He's this kid who writes with us for *The Hawk*. Elwin's really smart, Mom. He wrote this terrific story about a boy who's always been homeschooled and never went to public school before."

"It sounds to me as if you like Elwin, Calliope."

"I do, Mom. Not *like*-like. Not like a boyfriend or anything. But anyway, Elwin isn't what's wrong. I mean, it's what some other kids do to him. There's this kid, Junior, he calls Elwin a mouse—because he's small—and rags on him all the time. Today, I saw Junior shove Elwin against the wall—hard. And he does other things, like snatching Elwin's hat or his lunch. But Elwin never fights back. He just takes it.

"I guess he really couldn't fight back. Elwin has asthma. And Junior is this big lump. Today, he had a couple of other kids with him. They all thought it was funny, shoving Elwin, but it wasn't."

"And you're wondering, Calliope, what you should do."

"Yeah. It's really tough. I almost want to get in Junior's face about it, but if I do, it'll make things worse for Elwin—a girl defending him."

"You could report it, Calliope."

"No, I can't do that, either. That would only make Elwin look bad, like he had a friend do his ratting for him."

"It seems to me that Junior is the real rat. You're in quite a bind, Calliope."

"I am, Mom. And I was hoping you'd tell me what to do."

"Some problems, sweetheart, don't have easy solutions. This one certainly doesn't. If you were Polly's age, I'd go right to school and have a talk with the teacher. But you're not a little girl now, and I can't do that. All I can tell you, Calliope, is to go on being a friend to Elwin. He needs his friends to help keep him strong."

"That's it, Mom? Just be Elwin's friend? I don't think he is my friend. Not yet, anyway. I mean, we're both on *The Hawk*. But I don't do stuff with him, like after school."

"Would you like to be Elwin's friend, Calliope? When I asked you if you liked Elwin, you said you did. But not '*like*-like,' you said." And my mother gives me one of her mom-smiles. "So if he isn't a friend, what is he?"

My mother's always doing that. I ask her for help, and instead she asks me a question. And waits until I come up with an answer. And she's doing it right now.

"You think I should try to be Elwin's friend?"

"It's not what I think, Calliope. If you want to be Elwin's friend, then go ahead and be his friend."

"How do I do that? This isn't first grade, Mom. I can't just walk up to Elwin and say, 'Do you want to be my friend? I'll trade sandwiches with you.'"

"That's true, Calliope. But you're smart, and you're resourceful. I'm sure you'll figure it out."

Callie's Rule:
- When parents tell you to figure out something for yourself, it's usually because they don't know the answer.

13 Squirrels and Smokes

I still don't have an idea for another story, a story that even those kids who never read anything but the sports page will be certain to hear about, a story that Mr. Fischer will never forget. But even though my eyes and my ears are everywhere, even though my brain is scrabbling through every possibility, like a squirrel searching for buried acorns, I don't find a thing.

Now I'm sitting at a table in the Hawk's Nest, still searching, when Mr. Fischer suggests that some of the kids might write about people who work at our school—teachers, librarians, office assistants. (Not the principal!) And then it hits me.

My big idea is that I ought to interview a janitor. Mr. Fischer wants us to interview someone at school. No one else is going to think of interviewing a janitor. I already know Buzz Henwick; I interviewed him for the cockroach story (now the dead cockroach story). And, of course, I'm good at interviews.

And in a little dark corner of my brain, I'm thinking that Buzz Henwick might be mad at Mr. No-Man for kicking him out of his smoking room. I'm starting to like Buzz Henwick.

This could turn out to be a very good story. My really great story will have to wait.

So here I am, waiting by the janitor's closet for Buzz Henwick. My father lent me the tiny Dictaphone from his office. "Callie," he said, "if you record the interview, you'll be sure to quote accurately." (See, Dad? I just quoted accurately.) Here comes Mr. Henwick now, wheeling his cart with the mops and brooms and stuff.

"Mr. Henwick?"

He's a tall, skinny man, and I have to tilt my head back to talk to him. The next twenty minutes are not at all what I expected. I think my recording can explain it better. Here's what I have.

C. *Mr. Henwick?*

B. *You can call me Buzz.* (He's putting away his brooms and mops and pail.)

C. *Buzz, do you remember me? I asked you about the cockroach in the girls' locker room?*

B. *Yeah, I remember. Look, if them cockroaches is back, it ain't my problem. The exterminator gave me a guarantee. Call him. I keep a clean building. Anyone's got any complaints, let 'em call him. He's got some crazy name—oh, yeah, the X-Terminator. Call him.*

C. *No, I wasn't asking about the cockroaches. This is for another story. I wanted to write about you for the new school newspaper.*

B. *You from that newspaper?* (I'm standing in the doorway, and Buzz turns toward me.)

C. *Yes, I am.*

B. *I ain't got nothin' to say to you.*

C. *But, Buzz, I haven't asked you anything yet.*

B. *I said, I ain't talkin' to you. Not to nobody from that paper.*

C. *Why?*

B. *Why? You want to know why? I'll tell you why. Me and Tom, we work hard. We're on our feet all day cleanin' up the messes you kids make. You spill somethin' in the lunchroom, you gonna clean it up? No way. Call Buzz, he'll do it for you. Kid pukes? Call Buzz. Writing on the bathroom walls? Call Buzz. A bunch of spoiled babies, that's what you are. So all we got, Tom and me, all we got is a little room where we can sit down, have a smoke. Course, we don't have it no more. We brought us in a couple of chairs, a little TV— it was nice. We'd go in there, sit down, have a smoke . . .*

C. *But that was the problem. There's no smoking allowed in the school.*

B. *We wasn't smokin' in the school; we was smokin' in our room.*

C. *That was still in the school. Besides, smoking is bad for your health. You know that. It's better for you if you don't smoke.*

B. *Now we got to go clear down to the corner if we want a smoke. Just takes more time, that's all.*

C. *You shouldn't smoke at all. You should quit.*

B. *You think I didn't try? Been smokin' for thirty years. Probably tried quittin' maybe ten, fifteen times. Nothin'. Still smokin'. Look, kid, I work hard all day. Only thing gets me through the day is thinkin' in a little while I'll go in there, sit down, have a smoke, take it easy. Now I ain't got that no more. Now I got to wait till lunch. Just makes it harder to get my work done, that's all. Look, kid, I got nothin' to say to you. I just want to get out of here and go home. So I can sit down and have a smoke.*

I don't have a story. Again. I thought Buzz would be mad at Mr. No-Man. Maybe he is, but he's also mad at us. At me. Though Buzz did get me thinking. About how hard his job is. And how we sometimes make it harder for him. But there's no story in that. I'm just going to have to keep scrabbling.

14 Questions and Answers

So I'm sitting on my bed, scrabbling in my brain for another idea, and I just keep coming up with nothing. My father said I was good at interviews. Boy, was he wrong. The interview with Buzz the janitor was a complete wreck. The interview with Chief Bloodworth didn't go so great, either. A lot of the parts I put into the story got taken out. The only good part of the interview that got printed was the part where I asked Chief about the evacuation drills. I remember I said, "Sometimes kids will call in about a fake bomb—you know, to get out of a test or something. Or even just for a joke." But when we wrote it, my question got left out. The only thing left in was Chief's saying that kids who do that are just "abetting the terrorists." As though he just happened to mention that. I didn't get any credit for asking the question in the first place.

Probably the only thing that I'll ever have printed in a real newspaper is my obituary.

> *Calliope Jones died a complete failure, never having achieved her goal of becoming a newspaper reporter. When asked to remember something significant about his daughter, Calliope's father, Herman Jones, thought for some moments, then he said, "I did, at one time, think she was good at interviewing people. But I may have been mistaken."*
>
> *During her short lifetime, Ms. Jones published only one story, a piece that she cowrote with Shane Belcher. Mr. Belcher recalled that working with Calliope was sometimes difficult. "She always had a lot of opinions," he said.*

Hey, hold up, stop the presses. Opinions. I do have a lot of opinions. I don't need Shane to remind me of that. And I sure don't need Shane to be sarcastic after I'm dead. But I just remembered something—the third page of the paper, the place where people could express their opinions. Well, I've got lots of opinions, and now they're bopping around in my brain like in a pinball machine. Flashing lights and colors everywhere.

And suddenly, one giant flash. All those good ideas I had about the interview with Chief, the parts that didn't get published, I can put all of those into my opinion piece. Not what Chief said, of course. Especially not the part about the metal dog tags. No, this piece is going to be just about what I think.

I'd better write all this down before I forget some of it.

> *Everyone thinks school has too many requirements.*

Good opening, Callie. Last year, my English teachers used to tell us "think about who your audience will be and write as though they're listening to you." Well, I can't imagine a single middle-school kid who won't be listening now.

For example, girls don't think they should be required to take sewing.

Oops. Don't want Miss Stern on my case, too. Better change that.

For example, some *girls don't think they should be required to take sewing. And everyone complains about having to do homework over school vacation. But there is one requirement that most students have not considered. And they should, because this is a requirement that is completely useless.*

(As though sewing class isn't even more useless.)

That requirement is the school evacuation drill, which is not only useless but also dangerous.
Those drills are dangerous because, if there were a real bomb explosion in the school, flying building parts could seriously injure students, who would be standing just outside in the parking lot.

I should give Shane credit here, but I won't.

The drills are useless because if a terrorist were to plant a bomb inside the school, they wouldn't text or email the school and tell everyone to get out. What would be the point of that? But kids do make those threats sometimes, to get out of taking a test, or on a dare, or just because they're fooling around.

And those fake bomb threats aren't just useless, they're dangerous, too—dangerous to the kids who make them, because they're breaking the law.

Maybe I should change that last part—makes me sound too much like a grown-up. But I bet Mr. Fischer would like it. I'll leave it in.

If they're found out, they could get into real trouble, not just with the school, but with the police.

And finally, the school evacuation drills are a waste of time, our time. We're in school to learn, not to stand outside in the cold or the rain without our jackets, while the class period is running out. Just because one kid doesn't want to take a test doesn't mean that the whole school has to suffer.

Uh-oh. Stop for a minute, Callie. Are you thinking about your audience now? Are you seeing all those kids who don't think they're suffering if they can get out of a boring class? All those kids who actually cheer when the alarm goes off? Who don't care if it's real or fake as long as it wastes some time?

I'm seeing my audience now. I'm seeing me on one side of a football field and the entire school lined up against me on the other side, yelling at me. Well, it won't be the first time. And if I can save even one kid from getting hit by exploding bomb parts or getting arrested for calling in a fake bomb scare, then it'll all be worth it.

I need a really strong ending. What . . . ? Got it.

So I think it's time to blast the bomb drills.

I think a piece like this deserves a rule.

Callie's Rule:

- A good reporter has to tell the truth, even if she is taking a big risk.

I'm finished. And my piece is 277 words. That's longer than any of the front-page articles. No way anyone will miss this one.

It seems like a lifetime before the next issue of *The Hawk* appears, but it's finally here, with my article taking up most of page three. And it looks as if no one in the whole school has missed this one. All day long the kids keep coming up to me, whining and arguing about my piece.

"Geez, Callie, what's with you? You like sitting in school all day?"

"Get a life, Callie!"

"I bet you'd rat on someone who phoned in a bomb scare, wouldn't you?"

And on and on. And over and over. I've heard those same things so many times that when Shane comes up to me, I practically scream at him, "Of course I'd rat someone out. Just so I can sit through one more boring history class."

"Cal, have you gone nuts or something? I just wanted to tell you that I thought your piece was really good."

"You mean it? That's what you were going to say?"

"I was, but now I'm not so sure."

"Sorry, Shane. It's just that everybody else in this whole entire school seems to think I'm some kind of suck-up."

"You? Boy, do they not know you, Cal."

We both start to laugh. And right now that feels really good.

15 Threats

I've been called down to the principal's office. Right in the middle of English class.

What's going on? They call you down to the office only if you've done something bad. Or if something bad has happened . . . No, I won't think about that. I can't think about that. It's got to be something I've done. But what? I've never been in trouble in school. I never, ever do bad stuff. At least not in school. Oh, sure, I think lots of bad stuff, but I never do it. Mr. No-Man can't possibly know what I've been thinking. He's not some kind of mind-reading alien . . . He isn't, is he?

My hands are shaking so hard I can't even stuff my books into my backpack. Everyone's staring at me. I can feel their eyes on my back.

My knees are wobbly, and I have to clutch

the railing to keep from falling down the stairs.

The secretary's asking me something.

"Excuse me?"

"I asked your name. What is your name?"

"Callie . . . Calliope . . . Jones."

She opens the door to the principal's office and turns back to me.

"Principal Nolan is waiting for you."

Principal Nolan is sitting behind his desk and looking straight at me. He doesn't say anything, doesn't even blink.

The door opens again, and Mr. Fischer walks in. Oh, no. This has something to do with *The Hawk*. I've done something terrible, and Mr. Fischer had to report me to the principal. I think I could live with Mr. No-Man being angry with me. I'm pretty certain I could. Even if he suspended me, I could live with that. But if Mr. Fischer thinks I've done something bad, if he's disappointed in me . . .

Mr. Fischer smiles at me, not a happy-to-see-you smile, more of an I'm-feeling-a-bit-uncertain-so-I-don't-know-what-else-to-do smile. I know exactly how he feels.

Mr. No-Man gets up and goes to the door. "Ms.

Hernandez, would you bring in another chair, please?"

I'm really glad for that chair. I don't think my legs would hold me up one more second.

"Mr. Fischer," Mr. No-Man says, "I thought you ought to be here today when I speak with Calliope. I want to discuss something that she wrote for the school newspaper. The newspaper, Mr. Fischer, for which you serve as adviser."

It *is* something I've done. And in about three seconds, Mr. Fischer is going to know what it is. I wish that I did.

"Calliope, I believe that you wrote an article about the school security drills, did you not?"

"Principal Nolan," Mr. Fischer says before I have a chance to answer, "you know that she did. Could we please get to the point? I have a class waiting."

"Yes, of course. Calliope, in your article, you voiced a number of complaints about those drills. And now I've been receiving those same complaints from parents. The parents are worried that their children are being made to stand out in the cold or the rain, that their children are missing out on essential class time. In short, Calliope, the parents had no such concerns until they read your article."

"I'm sorry, Principal Nolan," Mr. Fischer says, and he doesn't sound sorry at all, "but I don't see what you're getting at. The parents are concerned about the problems that Callie wrote about. She didn't create the problems; she only reported on them."

Hey, Mr. Fischer is right. I was only doing what a good reporter does. I found a problem, and I wrote about it. I can't possibly be in trouble for that.

"Mr. Fischer," Mr. No-Man says, and he's looking rather grim. Not that he doesn't always look grim, but he looks grimmer than usual. "Mr. Fischer, you seem to be forgetting why we have a school newspaper. It was decided that we would publish a newspaper for several reasons. We thought that writing for a newspaper would help the students develop their writing skills. But we also thought that the newspaper would present a positive image of the school, that it would convey to the entire school—students, teachers, staff, and parents as well—information about all the good things that are occurring here. Instead, I find articles about cockroaches in the girls' locker room and the detrimental effects of security drills. I was able to remove the cockroach fiction from the paper, but when this second article came up, I was occupied with preparing the school budget. Had I seen it, I never would have permitted it."

Mr. Fischer stands up. His hands are clenched. And when he speaks, his voice is low.

"Principal Nolan, we are publishing a school newspaper, not a public relations puff piece. I'm teaching the students that they must always write the facts, truthfully and fully. Callie's article fit that standard, and so I approved it. If you have a problem, Principal Nolan, it's with me, not with Callie."

"No, Mr. Fischer, I do have a problem with Calliope. A very serious problem. And it's something that needs to be discussed further."

"In that case, Principal Nolan, I believe that Callie's parents ought to be here with her."

"Quite right. Calliope, please tell your parents that I'll expect them here tomorrow, after school, in my office."

● ● ●

I can't. I can't tell my parents. Maybe I could transfer schools or something. Tell them I'd have much better educational opportunities somewhere else. Or even better, say that I want to be home-schooled. I have all my books and my assignments. My mom could supervise me. That's it. I'll tell them I want to be homeschooled.

I'm going to need some really good reasons for that. It's so hard to argue with my parents. They're always asking me for reasons. And my father likes to ask me for proof. Like he's a detective, not a lawyer.

Okay, so I'll make a list of my reasons.

1. The gym teacher is a sadist. Proof: She makes us go outside for softball even when it's thirty-five degrees.
2. The cafeteria is a zoo at lunch. I'm getting an ulcer just from the noise and confusion. Proof: A gnawing pain in my left side. (Could that be appendicitis?) Okay, make that my right side.

3. School starts much too early, and I'm not a morning person. If I were homeschooled, it would be better for my biorhythms.
4. The school is just a kettle of contagion. Everyone's coughing and sneezing and blowing their noses. If I stay there, I'll miss most of the winter being sick.
5. I would really like to study Latin and my school doesn't offer it. (Not such a good reason. If I do get homeschooled, my mom might make me study Latin.) How about Chinese instead? Now that I could probably use.

Right. Like any of those reasons will convince them. I'll just have to tell them the truth. I do know one thing. My folks aren't one bit as scary as Principal No-Man.

16 Principals and Principles

My parents are waiting for me outside the office. (My homeschooling idea didn't rate more than a couple of raised eyebrows before my mother said, "All right, Calliope, suppose you tell us what's going on.") My mother puts an arm around me. Right in the middle of the school. If this were any other day, I'd try to squirm away before anybody saw us, but this isn't any other day. Today, if I could, I'd crawl into her lap.

Mr. Fischer hurries over, and we go in together. Last night, my mother told me to take a positive attitude. As the grown-ups are introducing themselves, I try to think of something positive. Well, first of all, there are four of us, and Mr. No-Man's only one person. Second, my father's a lawyer. But Mr. No-Man is a principal—my principal.

Callie's Rule:

- Even if your father's a lawyer, at school, the principal is the law.

.But when we go into the office, I get a real shock. Mr. No-Man's not the only person waiting for us. Sitting next to his desk is Chief Bloodworth. I'm beginning to wish I was wearing one of those metal dog tags he talked about. I have the feeling that when this is all over, that tag will be all that's left of me.

"Let's get started, shall we?" Mr. No-Man says. "It seems we have something of a problem here—"

My father interrupts. "I'd like to know exactly what that problem is. From what I've been told, I don't see that there is one."

"Why don't I let Chief Bloodworth explain," Mr. No-Man says.

"Thank you, Principal Nolan, I will. Mr. Fischer," Chief says, "it really isn't necessary for you to be here today; you may leave if you'd like."

"No, Chief Bloodworth. I believe I ought to be here."

"As you wish, but I want to talk to Callie about a story that was printed in *The Hawk* about the school evacuation drills."

"Look," Mr. Fischer jumps in, "if you're concerned about that article, you don't need to be. Callie and Shane wrote it together, and I checked their notes thoroughly. I believe that they quoted you accurately. I can give you a copy of the article."

"No, thank you. I've seen the paper. In fact, I've seen every issue of the paper. My son Junior is a student at this school, and he brings them all home."

Junior. Chief said his son is called Junior. Of course, they even look a little bit alike, with that big body and those short legs. Does he know what a monster his kid is?

"No," Chief is saying, "it's another article that I'd like to talk about. Callie, you wrote something—an opinion piece, I think it was—didn't you?"

"Y-Yes."

"And in your article . . . I have it here. . . ."

Chief reaches into his pocket and pulls out a folded paper.

"In your article, Callie, you say that some students are making bomb threats. You wrote that they did it"—Chief looks down at a copy of the newspaper and reads from it—"'to get out of taking a test, or on a dare, or just because they're fooling around.' Now, of course, I've known that students have been making false threats. But I don't know exactly who is responsible. Do you know who those students are, Callie?"

"What do you mean?"

"Do you know their names? They're breaking the law. I need to know who they are. What are their names, Callie?"

Chief is staring hard at me. At least I think he is. I can't see his eyes behind those eye slits.

"I—I don't know. I only know that kids do it. Everybody knows that. When the alarm goes off, people laugh and say, 'Someone's getting out of a test.'"

"I'm not interested in what other people say. Other people didn't write the article, *you* did. I must warn you, Callie, that if you're protecting someone, you could be in serious trouble."

No, *no*. This isn't happening. It can't be

happening. Chief's a bully, just like his son. Junior bullies with his hands, but Chief bullies with his words. I look at my father for help, but he doesn't look back. He's glaring at Chief.

"I must warn *you,* Chief Bloodworth, that it sounds as if you're threatening my daughter. You are on dangerous ground right now."

For a moment, Chief looks startled. But only for a moment. "You're right, of course, Mr. Jones. I didn't mean to accuse your daughter. But she does need to answer some questions. Callie wrote that she knew students who were making false bomb threats to the school."

"Wait just a minute, Chief Bloodworth," Mr. Fischer says. "Callie never wrote that she 'knew' those students. She never even said that she knew who they were. She only wrote that she knew that students do make false threats."

My father is nodding his head.

Chief's face is getting a little red. "That may be true, but I believe Callie knows the names of those students, and she's refusing to tell me who those students are. I think she's protecting her friends."

Protecting my friends. But I don't. I can't. I can't protect Elwin from Junior. And now I can't protect myself from his father. I suddenly feel small, like a little kid sitting in a grown-up chair.

"Chief Bloodworth," my father says. He's speaking in his lawyer voice, the one I hear when he's talking to clients on the telephone. "I'd like to ask you a question, if I may. Are you aware that there has recently been a series of break-ins in town?"

"Yes, of course I know about them, but I don't see what they have to do with—"

"How do you know of them, Chief Bloodworth?"

"I'm in touch with the police—that's an important part of my job. It was the police who told me about the break-ins."

"And can you tell me who is responsible for those break-ins?"

"Of course not. No one's been arrested yet."

"I see. So you're saying that you know about the break-ins but you don't know who is responsible. Is that right?"

Chief doesn't answer. He's been stopped. My father stopped him. Dead in his seat.

Mr. Fischer is grinning; he doesn't even try to hide how pleased he is. My mother reaches over and lightly pats my father's hand. But Mr. No-Man doesn't look so happy. And Chief's not saying a word.

"Chief Bloodworth," my father says, "I believe you owe my daughter an apology."

"Well, all right. I suppose it is possible that Callie doesn't actually know the names of the students responsible. But I should warn you, young lady—"

"Chief," my father says, "if I were you, I'd be careful what I said right now."

"Yes," Mr. No-Man says. Wow, he's really saying yes, not no. That has got to be a first. My father stopped a bully. And he did it entirely with words.

"Well, it appears," Chief says, "that this matter is settled. And I must say that I'm glad to know that Calliope has not been deceiving us. But Mr. Fischer, if I may, I'd like to speak with you for a moment. Alone."

"Is this about the newspaper?" Mr. Fischer asks.

"Well, yes, it is."

"I think I know what you're going to say, Mr. Nolan. So why don't I say it for you. You are about to tell me that you think you should review *everything* that appears in the paper from now on, including letters and editorials. Is that right?"

"Well, as I've said before, the school newspaper reflects the school, and we certainly don't want the paper to reflect badly on the school."

"We talked about this yesterday, Principal Nolan. But you seem not to have understood me. And I'm afraid that, despite what I said, you don't quite understand the function of a newspaper. Or what I'm trying to teach the students. A newspaper prints the truth—whether it's good or bad. I won't let my students publish anything that's false or libelous, but what Callie wrote was neither. What she wrote was accurate and timely, and that's all I required."

What's happening? I don't understand.

"Well, my requirements, Mr. Fischer, are a bit broader than that. If you can't follow them, I'm afraid I'll have to suspend publication of your paper."

Mr. Fischer just looks at Mr. No-Man for a

minute. Then he says, "Fine." That's all he says, just "Fine."

Fine? It's not fine. Not fine at all. Mr. Nolan's going to shut down the paper. There won't be any more *Hawk*. This is all my fault. If I hadn't gotten so carried away with myself, hadn't written that stupid piece on the evacuation drills, we'd still have *The Hawk*, Mr. Fischer would still be our adviser, and I'd still be . . .

My father is saying something, but there's a ringing in my head so loud that I can't hear a word. He and my mother and Mr. Fischer are getting up, and I follow them, out of the office, out of the building.

When we're in the parking lot, Mr. Fischer stops and says, "I'm almost glad this happened."

Glad? How can he be glad? *The Hawk* is finished. There's no newspaper. I'm not a reporter. And I'm not in any group. It's all over.

I look at Mr. Fischer for a long time. This is the last time I'll see him, and I want to remember him. I wonder if he'll remember me.

"Callie," Mr. Fischer says, and I'm expecting he's going to say good-bye. "Don't give up just yet. I have an idea," he says, "and I'd like to talk to you about it—you and all the other kids on *The Hawk*. I wonder if we could get together someplace to discuss it."

"Of course," my mother says. "You could meet at our house. Would this Saturday be good for you?"

Oh no. My mother asked Mr. Fischer to come to our house. What will Mr. Fischer think? My mother likes the way our house looks. Of course she does, she decorated it (if you can call that decorating). I wonder if I could sort of redecorate. Maybe hide the barber's chair. And some of the other six kids. That'll be the bad part. But the good part, the very best of all part, will be that I'll be seeing Mr. Fischer again. If only for the last time.

17 Blue Quilts, Black Tumors, and a White Light

It's now two thirty on Saturday afternoon, and Mr. Fischer and all the kids from *The Hawk* are supposed to be here by three. I tried to redecorate, I really did. I mean, what is Mr. Fischer going to think when he sees our house? I can keep him out of most of the other rooms, but not the living room. The living room that doesn't have a sofa, chairs, and a coffee table, like what normal people would have. Nope. We've got a bunch of rocking chairs—they don't even match—and a red leather barber's chair in the place of honor. (It's my father's. When he's home, no one else is allowed to sit in it.) And a coffee table? No way. Our tables are things like a dentist's tray on top of a birdbath. And that's the best of them.

So for what must have been an hour, I tried to

push, shove, and drag the barber's chair out of the living room. I couldn't budge it. (Why don't they put wheels under those things?) It's probably just as well, since I have no idea where I would have put it if I could have gotten it out of the room. Anyway, when I saw that the barber's chair would have to stay, I thought maybe I could cover it up. So I pulled the blue quilt off my bed and threw it over the chair, tucking it in all around, hoping the quilt would look like a slipcover on a very big chair. It didn't. The barber's chair just looked like some hulking monster under a bed quilt.

I put the quilt back on my bed and tackled the other problem—keeping my brothers and sisters away. For this one, I decided that the direct approach was best: I first warned them all to stay out of the meeting. When a straight warning didn't seem to be getting through to them, I tried blackmail. I told them that I knew things on each of them that Mom and Dad would love to hear about. And that their absence would assure my silence. They sort of grumbled, but said they'd stay out.

I really wanted everything to be perfect for this

meeting. I mean, this will be the last time we'll ever be together. The Hawk's Nest is gone now— maybe I should go by on Monday and take down the sign—and after today, even *The Hawk* will be finished. No nest, no paper, no group. After today, the only thing left will be me, right back where I started.

The kids are all arriving. And—this is really amazing—they love the barber's chair. Especially the boys. They all want to sit in it. Andrik (he's kind of pushy) gets to the chair first, and he's sitting there, his legs crossed under him, looking like some pasha in the Ali Baba story, when Mr. Fischer walks in. After Mr. Fischer's said hello to everyone, he walks over to the barber's chair, stands in front of Andrik, and makes a scram sign, jerking his thumb over his shoulder.

"Okay, guy," he says, "I'm in charge here, and this chair is mine."

Andrik hunkers down on the floor next to Elwin and the other kids.

I guess it's time for me to bring in what my mother would call the refreshments. I spent the morning making popcorn and brownies and chocolate chip cookies. (Andy offered to help me make them from scratch, but I'd already bought the mixes, and anyway, I wanted to do it all myself.) So I've just brought in the cookies, and the guys are already scarfing down the popcorn, when Andy makes her appearance. She's carrying in the plate of brownies, as if she's trying to help (uh-huh!), but all the while, she's staring at Mr. Fischer. All the boys are staring at Andy. Mr. Fischer's the only one who's not. He really is wonderful.

I just manage to get Andy out of the room, when the twins show up. With plates. Big plates. They head right for the food, load their big plates, and leave. Without a word. For once, I'm glad they're kind of rude.

But when Polly comes in, there's no way *she's* going to keep quiet.

"Mommy says I can take one cookie," she says. "But I asked her if I could take a cookie and a brownie, and she said I could. So I can, Callie. Mommy said so."

Now the girls are cooing about how cute Polly is, and Polly is really lapping it up. She's about to make the rounds of all the girls, but I tell her that she got her treats and she has to leave. As I lead Polly out of the room, I notice Mel, standing just outside the doorway, trying to peek in. At Mr. Fischer. This is hopeless! I tell Mel she might as well come on in and get something to eat. And, of course, get a closer look at Mr. Fischer—but I don't say that.

That leaves only Jack unaccounted for. He probably thinks he's too mature to grub for treats, so we probably won't see him this afternoon. But as for the rest of them—well . . .

Callie's Rule:

- **Treats trump threats every time.**

"I think," Mr. Fischer announces, "we should get started. You all help yourselves to the food while we talk."

All right, Callie, face your fate. You've been pushing the ugly thing to the back of your mind, back behind barber chairs and brownies, but it was always there. All the time. Like some skulking brain tumor. Waiting. Waiting to kill you. In about thirty seconds all the kids will know that I'm the reason there won't be a *Hawk* ever again. They'll all know, and they'll all hate me.

I think tonight I'll have to bring up the home-schooling idea again.

"You're probably wondering," Mr. Fischer says, "why we're meeting here, instead of in school, and on a Saturday. Well, there's some bad news. I'm afraid *The Hawk* won't be the Hillcrest Middle School paper."

Everyone's talking at once, wanting to know why not, what happened. I'm just sitting there, frozen, waiting for the door to open and someone in scrubs and a white coat to walk in and tell me that I have only seconds to live.

"Okay, hold on just a minute," Mr. Fischer breaks in. "I know you're full of questions, but I'm afraid I'm not able to answer all of them. All I can say is that Mr. Nolan has decided to terminate publication of *The Hawk*."

"No more paper?" Jamie wails.

"I didn't say that there wouldn't be a paper. I should have said that it won't be a school paper. You'll just have to trust me that I'm trying to do what is best for the paper and best for all of you."

Isn't he going to tell them why? That *I'm* the reason Mr. No-Man is shutting down the paper? Is it possible, just barely possible, that I'm not going to die? Or at least not today? But don't get your hopes too high, Callie. Don't give up on that homeschooling proposal just yet.

About a zillion questions are flying around the room, but Mr. Fischer holds up his hand for silence. "I think I can answer most of these questions. Just wait a minute. Some of you may remember that at our first meeting, I told you that the future of newspapers would probably not be in print. Well, I think you people can be part of the future of newspapers—if you want to be. I'd like to have you publish *The Hawk* online. What do you think?"

Of course, everyone is thinking—and saying— yes to that idea. I don't say anything. I'm looking at Mr. Fischer, and he looks to me as though a white light is shining all around him.

"Now, it might take me a little while to get the site up and running. I'm not terribly good at these things, but I have a friend who works in computers, and he's offered to help. Once the site is up, everyone at HMS will be able to read the paper online."

Everyone. Even Mr. No-Man. Of course. But now there won't be a thing he can do to stop us. I don't think. But I don't care. I don't whoop-de-doo care. *The Hawk* is back, the group is back, I'm back. Life is good.

"There is the matter," Mr. Fischer says, "of the name. What should our online paper be called?"

"Mr. Fischer," Elwin says, "I really like the name Callie thought up, but we could just put an *e* on the end of the name, because it'll be electronic now. Call it *The Hawke*, H-a-w-k-e."

Everybody likes that idea. People start saying that the name will look really cool, sort of like a name for a superhero.

"Okay, then. We've got our new name."

Our name—Elwin's and mine.

"Now, what I'm about to say is very important. When *The Hawk*, no final *e*, was a school news-paper, I was your adviser. That was part of my job, working with you as an extracurricular activity. I guess my role will be a little bit different now. Clearly, being adviser to an online paper is not part of my job description. But this is something I really want to do. I've seen how enthusiastic and serious you are about your work. So if you all are willing to put in your own time, I don't see why I can't volunteer my own. Is that okay with all of you?"

Of course, everyone agrees.

"Thank you. Now, since we don't have to worry about printing costs," Mr. Fischer says, "we can make *The Hawke*, with a final *e*, as long or as short as we like. So if we want to run extra stories, or additional letters or editorials, we can do that. And on weeks when we have fewer submissions, we can have a shorter edition.

"There will also be some changes to the paper. Can we call it a paper if it's not printed on paper? I guess not. One change—and I know you won't be unhappy about this one—is that we won't have to print lunchroom menus or the school calendar. Also, if we're not an official school paper, you'll have a lot more freedom to include articles that might be critical of school matters."

Yes! If there's ever another cockroach incident, I can write about it.

"One thing won't change, however. Well, two

things, actually. Whatever you write will have to be the very best writing that you can do. And we'll still need to plan each issue together. Now we could do that online, but I'd still like us to meet, once every couple of weeks or so, because—maybe because I'm older than you—but I still believe in talking things out face-to-face. So we'll be having regular editorial meetings, just as we did before, only they won't be at the school."

The group! The group is really back!

"There is one more very small thing. When we were a school newspaper, our costs were covered by the school. But we're on our own now. The costs won't be very great, mostly the cost of the site, but we will still have to think of a way to pay for them. Any ideas?"

"How about," Shane says as he helps himself to popcorn with one hand and a fistful of cookies with the other, "we have a bake sale? We could run one easy. Bake sales can sell a lot of stuff. Everyone likes cookies."

"Yeah," Jamie says, "look at us?"

Mr. Fischer puts it to a vote, and everyone is in favor of our running a bake sale.

"Okay, but where will we have it?" Alyce wants to know. "Can we have the bake sale at the school, Mr. Fischer? In the cafeteria would be perfect."

"No, Alyce. We can't do that. *The Hawke* isn't part of the school now. Any other suggestions?"

"It's got to be indoors, at least until the spring."

"And it'll have to be someplace where there're a lot of people."

"That barber's chair got me thinking?" Jamie says. "My mom has a hair salon? She gets a lot of customers there every day? And I know she'd let us do it in her place? I'll ask her, but I know she'll say yes?"

"Just don't put the table near the chairs," Shane says. "We won't sell too many cupcakes with hair frosting."

"Or frosted hair."

We're all going a little bit nuts now, and Mr. Fischer cuts in.

"Okay, people, I think we've done enough planning for today. One bake sale should cover our costs for the rest of the year. I'll leave it to you kids to plan it. We should meet again next week so we can start discussing story ideas for our first online issue. Be ready with your ideas. I'm going to pass around a sheet of paper, and I'd like each of you to write down your email address. Since we can't meet at the school from now on, I'll set up a listserve so that we can keep in touch. Callie, will it be all right if we meet here again next week?"

All right? It'll be brilliant. But I don't say that. I just say, "Fine." I'll have to ask my folks, of course, but they saw how Mr. Fischer stood up to Mr. Nolan—"defending his principles," my father would say—they'll be happy to have the meetings here.

As everyone is leaving, Alyce says that she'll bring the food next time. But I somehow don't think that, for me at least, the food is going to be the most important thing.

18 From the Outside In

Alyce is a half hour early for the next meeting. She's made cupcakes, with different color frosting and a little heart on each one. In seconds, the twins scuttle in, like ants at a picnic. I slap their hands away and shoo them out of the room. Those cupcakes must be sending out signals because everyone's coming early. When we're all here, sitting on the floor—scarfing down the cupcakes—and Mr. Fischer is in the barber's chair, I look around and suddenly see our living room in a way I never saw it before. I see a bunch of different rocking chairs and a bunch of different kids. But somehow the rockers all seem right together. And so do the kids.

Everyone is pretty excited—maybe they're on a sugar high—and they're all wanting to talk at once.

Mr. Fischer quiets them down and asks us to raise our hands to speak. He calls on Jamie first, I guess because she's usually pretty quiet.

"I have a question?"

Of course she does. Everything Jamie says is a question.

"If this isn't going to be a school paper anymore, can we write about anything we want?"

Most of the kids seem to like that idea, but Shane doesn't.

"If we write about anything we want," he says, "then we're just a bunch of bloggers, not an online news source. I think we have to stick to school stories, make this a paper about Hillcrest Middle School."

Shane's wrong. Utterly and completely wrong. I don't wait to be called on. I just burst out, "Shane, how is that different than what we did before? It'd be the same paper, only online."

"Except," Andrik says, "Mr. Nolan doesn't have to look at everything we write and say it's okay."

Alyce is waving her hand wildly. "Can we get in trouble if we write something that Mr. Nolan doesn't like?"

"Boy," Jamie says, "then we ought to quit right now?"

"Why?"

"Because Mr. No-Man doesn't like anything."

Wow, Jamie said that without a question mark at the end.

Everyone goes quiet. It was Mr. No-Man who shut down our paper in the first place, and even though he can't do that now, we're all just a little bit worried.

"I don't know about you guys," Andrik says, "but I'd like to write something that *would* get Mr. No-Man mad."

Elwin's just been listening so far, but now he says, "What would be the point, Andrik? I mean, think about it. Is that news? Mr. No-Man getting mad?"

Everyone has to laugh at that one.

"Wait," Elwin says, "I'm not finished. When Alyce said that about Mr. No-Man, it got me thinking. About the time Mr. Fischer asked us all to write up some complaints we had about the school. We sort of did it for fun, but now—now that we're not a school paper—we really can write about things that we think are wrong at school."

"Hey, you're right," Shane says. "We could do sort of investigative journalism. You know, expose problems at the school."

"Like that kids could get hurt," I say, "if there really were a bomb explosion at the school. We could write about stuff like that."

"Or"—Shane's grinning now—"about cockroaches in the girls' locker room."

"No, Shane. I'm serious. I know Mr. No-Man wouldn't let us print my cockroach story, but it was a real problem."

"I think I ought to jump in here," Mr. Fischer says. "Shane's first point was a good one, that your stories should concern the school. *The Hawke* needs to have a distinct focus. But what you people are saying now is also right: you need a purpose, something that will make the paper significant, that will make people want to read it. And that purpose, as you kids were saying, will be to take a different perspective on the school, to be critical if you need to be, to raise questions. Even if you don't yet have the answers."

Jamie raises her hand again. "I have a question?

I mean, I'm not sure if this would be something I could write about, but I'm a vegetarian, and most days I have to bring my lunch to school? I mean, even the pizza has pepperoni on it? Could I write about that?"

"Hey," Andrik says, "consider yourself lucky. Some of that cafeteria food might even make *me* a vegetarian."

"Maybe," Shane says, "that's their plan. Make the whole school go vegetarian—and healthier."

"Jamie," Mr. Fischer says, "That's an excellent idea for an article. And just the kind of thing I think *The Hawke* should be doing. Pointing out problem areas, but doing it in a constructive way. We don't just want to be critical. We basically want to show how things at the school could be made better. Why don't you kids give it some thought, see what you can come up with. Then have some ideas ready for our next meeting."

"Mr. Fischer," Alyce asks, "will you have to approve our stories before we put them in?"

"Yes, I will. But I'm going to apply a very different standard than Principal Nolan did. So I guess that pretty much wraps it up for today.

Is there anything else you kids think we need to settle?"

"Yeah," Andrik says, "who's bringing the food next time?"

All of us, even Mr. Fischer, say, "You are!"

We really are a group.

19 Equal-Opportunity Suffering

We may be a group, but I have to come up with a story idea on my own. And I know one thing for sure. I definitely, certainly, beyond—as my father would say—a shadow of a doubt, will not write about anything that could get me in trouble. Even if Mr. No-Man can't stop our paper, I still have to go to school every day. And I don't think it would be a good idea to get him mad at me again.

I really don't want anyone else mad at me, either. That eliminates most of the ideas the kids had thought of at that last meeting at school. For example, I can't write about any of the complaints about the janitors, like that they use a really strong disinfectant in the bathrooms or that during the vacation they waxed the chairs to the floors. I'm already in trouble with Buzz Henwick.

If I make him even madder, who knows what he could do to me. Maybe trip me up with his mop in the hallway. Or hang an OUT OF ORDER sign on the girls'-room door when I really need to use it.

Also, I can't write about any of the complaints I thought of about teachers. Like when I told my parents that the gym teacher was a sadist who sent us out to play ball in thirty-five-degree weather. If I write that, she'd probably send me out when it was down to fifteen degrees—all by myself.

No, this time, I've got to write something that will not only *not* get me into trouble but might even score me some brownie points. With teachers and kids.

It's been two days, and I haven't come up with a single good idea. And then I do. I really like this idea and I start to write immediately. I call it: "Unisex Sewing."

I really wanted to call it "Universal Suffering," but that was just asking for trouble. Anyway, here's what I've written:

Hillcrest Middle School requires that

all girls take a semester of sewing for each of their three years. Sewing is a valuable skill, and the girls learn a great deal in these classes.

Sure, like how to sew a blouse when no one even wears blouses now. At least not the kind you sew yourself. When they read this, the girls will probably be calling me a suck-up, or even worse, but if they read to the end of the article, they'll be cheering for me.

In fact, sewing is such a valuable skill that I think it should be taught to boys, as well as to girls.

Now all the boys are probably swearing at me. But read on, boys, before you click back to your video game.

There are many reasons why this class should be taught to both boys and girls. First, Hillcrest Middle School does not discriminate against girls, but when the school only allows girls to take a class, it is discriminating against boys.

A second reason is that many of the best-known fashion designers are men, and they earn a great deal of money. If boys don't learn to sew in school, they may miss out on opportunities to become rich and famous. Sewing classes may be just what they need to launch them into their future careers.

At this point, I think some of the boys— not most of them, but some of them—may be starting to take this idea seriously. Of course, they don't know what I really have in mind. Here it comes:

Now, the school has only one sewing teacher, Miss Stern. And even though Miss Stern is an excellent teacher . . .

Okay, so I am sucking up. Face it, I'll need all the help I can get when I take sewing again next year.

. . . she already is teaching a full schedule of classes. And there is no money in the school budget to hire another sewing teacher.

For which we should all be grateful.

So I propose that half of Miss Stern's classes be for boys and the other half for girls.

Which means, of course, that I, and every other girl in school, will have to take only half as many sewing classes. Instead of three semesters of sewing, we'd have only one and a half. The girls have got to be cheering for me by now. And the boys? Well, they've had it easy so far. Let them suffer a little.

Now I need a really strong conclusion. One that not even Mr. No-Man could disagree with. Here it is:

If Hillcrest Middle School is to remain an equal-opportunity educational institution, it must begin to offer boys the same

*opportunities for success as it offers to girls.
And that means the sewing classes should
be offered to everyone in the school—boys
as well as girls.*

Great job, Callie. In one stroke you've buttered up Miss Stern, won points with the girls, made an argument that even Mr. No-Man couldn't say no to, and proposed a way to get yourself out of a lot of sewing classes.

It's the next editorial meeting of *The Hawke*. Everyone's had a chance to read my article on the listserve, and they all have something to say about it. Alyce, of course, thinks it's a wonderful idea. She thinks boys would love to have a break from all those really boring classes like math. When she says that, Shane snorts. Alyce gives him a really annoyed look, but Shane pretends to cough and says that he took too big a bite of his cookie.

Andrik says, "You were kidding, right, Callie?"

I can't tell what I was really thinking, so I say, "No, I was serious. I think boys should take sewing just the same as girls. After all, girls have to have the same opportunities as boys, so it should work the other way around, too."

Callie's Rule:

• If you can't get out of a really dreadful requirement, you should try to share the pain.

20 Hemming and Hawing

I think I'd better scratch that last rule. When I wrote it, I had no idea how much pain I was going to have to share. My piece appeared in the first online issue of the paper, and lots of people read what I wrote about boys taking sewing. And, just as I suspected, most of the girls liked the idea. I even thought that some of the boys might like it. I just never thought that one of the boys would be a friend. And that that friend would ask me to help him get into Miss Stern's sewing class.

I need help myself. Alyce will know what to do. I mean, she loves the sewing class. She'll know what to do.

"Alyce, you won't believe what's happened."

"What? Something really cool? Tell me, Callie."

"I don't know how cool this is. Well, not for me it isn't. Maybe it's cool for Elwin. He wants to take Miss Stern's sewing class. Elwin says he wants to be a designer. He never told anyone before, but when he read my piece in *The Hawke,* he thought that it would really help him if he learned to sew. He said that this could be the start of his career."

"Elwin? Our Elwin? The one we know?"

"How many boys named Elwin *do* you know, Alyce?"

"I guess he's the only one. Ooh, Callie. This is so exciting. I can't believe it."

"I know. I can't believe it, either."

"I mean, our Elwin, someone we actually know, is going to be a fashion designer. Can't you just see it, Callie? Some famous star walking down the red carpet, with everyone watching, and they ask her, 'Who are you wearing?' And she says, 'Elwin. I'm wearing Elwin.'"

"Yeah, Alyce. I can picture it all now. Some famous star walking down the red carpet carrying Elwin on her back. Good thing he's small."

Alyce just stares at me for a moment.

Then she says, "Callie, you really don't know

anything. Elwin could be famous. And we'll be his friends. Maybe he'll let us wear his clothes sometimes or give them to us or . . ."

"I thought you'd be glad to know, Alyce. That's why I told you."

Well, Alyce was no help, no help at all. There's really no way out. I wrote the piece, Elwin took it seriously, and now I've got to go with him to ask Miss Stern if he can get into a sewing class.

So here we are, in that dreaded sewing room that lives on in my nightmares—the rows of monster machines, their metal teeth clacking and whirring, leaping off their tables and snatching at my clothes, catching them, catching me, pulling me down, down, down into their hungry guts.

Okay, Callie, get a grip. This isn't a nightmare; you're awake. You're here with Elwin, to help Elwin. So start helping.

"Miss Stern, I'm Callie Jones. You probably don't remember me"—I'm really hoping she doesn't—"I wrote the article for *The Hawke*—you probably didn't read it, it's online, but—"

"Yes, I did read it. I don't ordinarily read much on the computer, but your piece was brought to my attention, and I read it very carefully. I thought you made an excellent point, Callie."

"You did?"

"Yes, and you were quite right. There is no reason why boys shouldn't benefit from taking sewing classes just as girls do."

"Well, Miss Stern, this is Elwin. He wants to take sewing. This semester. But I'm not sure—"

"Elwin, it's a pleasure to meet you." Miss Stern is smiling, actually smiling, her mouth turned up instead of down. I hope she remembers all of this next fall, when I have sewing class again.

"Miss Stern," Elwin says, "I really would like to learn to sew. I have study hall for fifth period. I could give that up and take sewing then."

"Well, Elwin, the problem isn't so much *when* you could join a class, as *how.* You see, the classes are limited in size so that there is one machine available for each girl. However"—Miss Stern looks around the room—"the girls do not use their machines for the entire period. They also have to use the tables for cutting, pinning, basting, handwork, and so on."

As Miss Stern is saying all of this, Elwin looks as

if she's been reciting a menu of choices at a candy store.

"So it might be possible for the girls to share their machines with you. It wouldn't need to be just one girl. You could use whichever machine is free when you need it. Yes, I believe it could be done."

"Oh, Miss Stern, that would be great. Can I start this week?"

"I'm afraid not. This is unprecedented. Before I take you on as a student, you will have to get permission from Principal Nolan. Here, I'll write you a note, stating that I am willing to accept you in my class, provided that you first obtain Principal Nolan's permission. Take the note to him, and then bring it back to me when he's signed it."

Elwin wants to go immediately. But there's an obstacle in our way, a big, dumb obstacle who goes by the name of Junior. He's just coming out of detention when we leave Miss Stern's room.

"Hey, Elwin." He sneers. "How come you been in there? Wanted your girlfriend here to sew you something?"

"No," Elwin says, "I want to learn how to sew so I can sew your big mouth shut."

Wow! Good one, Elwin. He doesn't even wait for Junior's answer, just starts sprinting down the hall, with me dragging after him, toward the lair of the No-Man. By the time I get there, Elwin's already spoken to the secretary and made an appointment for the next day after school.

It's amazing how time flies ahead when you want it to go backward. It's already the next afternoon, and Elwin and I are standing outside Mr. No-Man's office door. I feel like we're Hansel and Gretel outside the witch's house. When we knock, I almost expect to hear a creaky voice say, "Who's that knocking at my door?"

But what I hear is that negative voice calling out, "Come in."

I start to explain why we're here, but Mr. No-Man cuts me off before I can finish.

"I've read what you've written, Calliope. Frankly, it's exactly what I would have expected from you. You seem to be constantly defying me, Calliope, trying to disrupt the orderly workings of this school. I can't allow one person, not you or anyone else, to upset the working order of Hillcrest Middle School."

Okay, that's it. I'm ready to leave.

But Elwin isn't. He starts at the beginning, that he wants to take the sewing class, that Miss Stern said there wouldn't be any problem, that she'd even written a permission slip for him. He hands the slip to Mr. Nolan.

"But." Mr. Nolan always begins his sentences with "but," the sentences that he doesn't begin with "no." "But the problem is not Miss Stern's to resolve. The problem is that if I let one boy take a sewing class, there will be others. Soon there will be a long line of boys wanting to take sewing. And there'll be no room for them. Oh, Miss Stern can possibly accommodate one boy—and I think it is admirable of her to take on an additional student—but it will be impossible for her to accommodate many boys.

"And then there is the area of equal opportunity. I believe you mentioned that in your piece, Calliope."

He fixes his laser eyes on me, as if he would like to liquefy me on the spot.

"I've already had to adjust the entire sports schedule to provide girls with the same teams that boys play on. Of course, that added significantly to the athletic budget. Now, if I allow one boy, and only one boy, to take a sewing class, then there will surely be protests, even civil suits, demanding that boys be treated equally with girls. Then I would have to hire an additional sewing teacher. And, of course, equip an additional room, and find money in the budget for all of that. Compared to which, the difficulty of scheduling the extra classes would be quite insignificant.

"No, Elwin. I cannot give you permission to take sewing. You needn't inform Miss Stern. I shall speak with her myself."

So I guess that's that. Elwin's really disappointed. But I tell him that he's still got the newspaper. And the Neighborhood Leisure Center offers sewing classes; he could take one there.

"Right. They're all about a hundred years old, and they'd call me 'Sonny.' No way. I think I'll ask for a sewing machine for my birthday and teach myself. But thanks anyway, Callie. You tried."

21 Courage

The worst thing has happened. Something much worse than masticating machines or negative No-Mans. There's been an incident at the school. Well, more than an incident. Last night, someone broke into the school through a basement window and smashed the glass in the door of the school secretary's office. Then they wrote in marker, on the outside of Mr. Nolan's door,

Mr Nolan Let me take soing
                                    Elwen

Of course, Elwin hadn't done it. (Geez, Louise, wouldn't Elwin at least spell his own name right?) No, it was Junior.

I'm mad, and when I get mad I want to tell

everyone. Or at least write something that everyone can read. My trusty computer awaits.

> *A terrible injustice was done today. The*
> *injustice was perpetrated by cowards, but it*
> *isn't the cowards who will suffer.*

I love that word—*perpetrated*—but I wonder
if it could be too dramatic. Maybe that whole
opening is too dramatic. I'd better start again.

> *Last night someone, or maybe several*
> *someones, broke into the office at Hillcrest*
> *Middle School and wrote an illiterate*
> *message on Principal Nolan's door. They*
> *wrote: "Mr Nolan Let me take soing." And*
> *they signed it, "Elwen."*
> *But their imprudent act betrayed them.*

No, I'm getting dramatic again. Better watch it.
Start those last sentences again, Callie.

> *Whoever wrote those words was try-*
> *ing to pin the blame on Elwin Watt, a*

seventh-grade student at the school who had asked if he could take a sewing class. You see, Elwin would like someday to be a clothing designer and, very sensibly, he thinks that sewing would be a useful and necessary skill for him to master. But for a variety of reasons . . .

I like that phrase—*a variety of reasons*—I'm not going to change it.

But for a variety of reasons, Elwin has learned that it won't be possible for him to take sewing at the school.

Now, that's not the whole story. All year, ever since he came to Hillcrest Middle School, Elwin Watt has been bullied. He's been pushed, shoved, tormented, and called nasty names. And Elwin took it all. He never cried, he never complained, he just took it. The bullies tried to break Elwin, but he never gave in. Elwin was tougher than the bullies.

So when the bullies learned about

Elwin wanting to take a sewing class, they thought that they had a perfect plan. They vandalized the office and scrawled a phony message, as though Elwin, in a fit of pique at being denied entrance to the sewing class . . .

Whoops, start that last part again.

as though Elwin was so angry at not being able to take sewing that he'd done the damage himself.

But the bullies were stupid, so stupid, and so careless, that they never bothered to learn how Elwin spells his name. It's Elwin with an i, *not an* e. *And, of course, Elwin does know how to spell* sewing. *The bullies don't. Which shows the bullies to be illiterate as well as stupid and cruel.*

So why does this matter? It matters because bullying doesn't just hurt the person being bullied. It hurts everyone. It hurts Elwin, of course, who has been humiliated. And it hurts the school janitor, Buzz

Henwick, who will have to sand down and refinish Principal Nolan's door and replace the glass on the office door.

And it hurts every student at Hillcrest Middle School. It hurts us because we're all afraid of the bullies. Maybe we go home every day and think how glad we are that it was someone else who got picked on. But we're still afraid because we know that tomorrow or the next day the bullies might decide to pick on us.

And someday they will. Unless we all stand up to them, together, and make them stop. Bullies are cowards. They'll gang up on one person, but they won't take on an entire school. It's up to all of us to make the bullies stop. When you see another kid being bullied, don't just look away. Say something, do something. Bullies are cowards. Stand up to them, and they'll back off.

So, that's what I write. And in a nanosecond, I've sent it to the entire staff of the paper. It's too late now for me to have second thoughts.

That night, I get an email from Mr. Fischer.

Callie,

Your article was a courageous piece of writing. It will be published right up front in our next issue of *The Hawke*. I doubt that we will ever be able to prove who the vandals were, but I think that maybe the best punishment for the guilty persons may be that their bullying days are over. If so, it will be thanks to what you wrote.

Keep writing what you believe, Callie. I know when I teach you kids about newswriting, I stress the importance of the facts. But I think that, for you at least, your beliefs may be even more important.

James Fischer

James. Mr. Fischer's name is James. I want to take that name and hold it against my heart, the way I used to hold my Raggedy Ann doll when I was small. James. James Fischer. James Fischer said my writing was courageous.

I'm not sure I'm so courageous. I'm okay when I'm writing, but when I'm face-to-face with someone, I'm maybe more hotheaded. When someone makes me mad, I usually blurt out whatever comes into my head. And I probably shouldn't do that.

Callie's Rule:

- Writing can sometimes be better than speaking. When you write something, you can read over what you wrote and change the wrong words for better ones.

22 Silent Words

Mr. Fischer has called a meeting, and he looks very serious. Not sad serious, just serious. Everyone's quiet, waiting.

"I've called this meeting today," Mr. Fischer says, "because there's something very important I need to tell you." But the way he says it tells us that this won't be a let's-give-a-shout-out-for-the-good-news announcement. Is it about Mr. Nolan? Is he trying to shut down our paper?

"I've always loved teaching. I love that a teacher can reach out to so many young people and touch their minds, even possibly change those young people in some way. But working with you has touched me, and has made me see teaching in a new way. What you all made me see is that journalism—in whatever form it may take in the future—can reach and influence countless minds, old as well as young. And sometimes, like teaching, it can change those minds."

What is Mr. Fischer trying to say? It sounds as though he's going to tell us what a wonderful job we've been doing, that *The Hawke* has reached a lot of people, and that some of what we've written has made a big difference. But that's not it. His face is too serious, not smiling the way it would be if he were simply going to congratulate us. No. He's going to say something we're not going to like, something I'm not going to like.

"What I'm trying to say—this is very difficult for me—just give me a moment."

Mr. Fischer swallows hard. He looks down at his hands. He can't look at us. He's leaving. I know it. Mr. Fischer is leaving us.

"I'll be leaving the school at the end of the semester. I've taken a job writing for an online news journal."

I feel the walls of the room caving in on me, smothering me, piercing my eardrums as they crash. And then it's over. I'm sitting on the floor of my living room, kids all around me, Mr. Fischer in front of me, but I'm nowhere and I'm alone.

I see the kids talking, asking Mr. Fischer questions, questions that he seems to be answering. I see him speaking to each of the other kids, but I don't hear anything. I don't say anything.

The other kids have left. There's only Mr. Fischer and me. I stand up and start to clear the dishes. I can't look at him.

"Callie." It's Mr. Fischer's voice. He's saying my name. I put down the plate I'm holding, afraid I might drop it.

"Callie, I know you're probably feeling abandoned, because you kids won't have me as the adviser for *The Hawke* next year. But I think you'll do just fine on your own. Callie, you've come a long way. The first piece you wrote for *The Hawk*, back when we were still a print newspaper—the cockroach story—was a fine piece of reporting and was well written. Even if it never did get published, you learned a lot doing it. But since that first article, your writing has grown, and you've grown. The last piece you wrote, about Elwin and the bullies, I think may well be one of the finest pieces of writing students at Hillcrest Middle School will ever read. It may have changed them. I know it changed me. It was when I read it that I realized what I wanted to do—what I've really always wanted to do—was to be a journalist. I only hope my writing can make as much of a difference as yours.

"Callie, I don't know what career you'll eventually decide on. But I'm hoping you'll become a writer."

A writer! Mr. Fischer is telling me to become a writer. Oh, I will, James Fischer, I will. And maybe, just maybe, I'll become a journalist. Like you.

23 Ripples

It's already May. Since that meeting, the one when Mr. Fischer said he'd be leaving, time has gone fast, too fast. Five more weeks and he'll be gone. I'd still like to do one more really important story before he leaves. But nothing's come up. Only the fashion show that I promised Alyce I'd write about with her. And I know for sure that that's not going to be anything important. But I told her I'd do it, and I have to.

The show is supposed to start at seven, but Alyce and I get to the school at six to watch the preparations. The girls are in the gym. They're all in their underwear—bras for almost all the girls, envious glances from the others—with their hair up in rollers, and the scene is as frenzied as a rock concert. Except that the sounds we're hearing, coming from the auditorium, aren't like any kind of rock I've ever heard. The band is rehearsing, and it sounds as if they could use a few more years of practice.

Alyce and I figure we should try to interview some of the girls, the way sportscasters do in the locker room before a game. Just as we approach an eighth-grader, we hear a scream. Everyone rushes over to see what's wrong.

"It's these stupid panty hose!" A sixth-grader with frizzy hair is sitting on a bench, yanking the torn panty hose off her foot. "I've just put my big toe through one leg, and there's a big hole in them. Now what do I do?"

"Don't ask me. I never wear those things."

"Me, neither. No one does."

"Except Miss Stern," a freckled girl says. "She said, 'No one will be permitted to appear in the fashion show unless she is wearing hose. And I shall be checking each one of you.'"

Everybody is laughing; she sounded exactly like Miss Stern. Everyone except the girl with the hole in her hose.

"Does this mean I can't be in the show?" Frizzy

Hair whines. "My mom and dad are both out there. If I don't go on—"

"It's okay," a tall blonde tells her. "My grandmother always carries a spare pair in her purse. She's small—they'd fit you. Grammy's probably out there already. She comes early for everything. One time she was an hour and a half early for a doctor's appointment. Said she'd been afraid of missing the bus."

"Oh no! I'd rather walk out there with a big hole on my leg than wear some grandmother's used support stockings."

"Not used. She always keeps a brand-new pair. Along with stomach mints, Scotch tape, manicure scissors, clear nail polish, a flashlight, her daily horoscope—"

"Okay, okay, I'll wear them. But not if they're support stockings. I won't wear support stockings. Could you ask her for me?"

"I can't! I'm in my underwear!"

Fuzzy Hair looks at me.

"You're dressed. Could you go?"

"I would," I say, "but I don't know her grandmother."

"That's easy," Tall Blonde says. "She'll be in the front row, and she'll be holding a giant purse on her lap. She never lets go of that purse. It's like her EMT bag."

When I come back with the emergency panty hose, the girls have started to put on their makeup. The eighth-graders have offered to do it for the sixth-graders, who are now sitting in a row, like birds on a telephone wire, waiting their turn.

The band's been quiet for a while, but now they start again. Well, some of them start. Some of the others are a half beat late.

That's pretty much how it goes—makeup, hair, clothes—until six forty-five, when Miss Stern comes into the gym and orders all the girls to line up in the hallway outside the auditorium and wait for their signals to go on.

The show proceeds exactly as I expected it would, the girls coming out in groups, sixth-graders first, modeling their skirts, then the seventh-graders with their tops, and finally the eighth-graders, who've made jackets. An eighth-grader announces each girl's name and describes her garment. Some of the girls look nervous, bewildered even, stumbling in with their group, forgetting to turn slowly when they reach the middle of the stage. But other girls look ready for their videos, smiling, strutting, spinning.

After about fifteen minutes, the band has played every song it has rehearsed, and they start to repeat the play list. They repeat it four times.

But the audience loves it all. Some of them cheer for their "girls," belting out their names with loud whoops. And they applaud for everyone.

The last girl has paraded her outfit, and people are getting up from their seats to head for the doors, when Miss Stern steps out on the stage.

"If I may ask you for just a few more moments of your attention, please."

The parents stop and turn toward the stage.

"We're all very proud of our girls this evening; they worked hard to create their garments, and so many other students worked to provide the music, the lighting, and the publicity posters for the show. They did everything they could to make this show possible. I'd like all of them to stand so we can applaud them."

The band members, the lighting people, the

audio kids, some kids who've been sitting in the audience scramble to their feet. It looks like half the school is standing. It probably is. Even the evil half—I see Junior with the band. He's behind the drums. It figures—he'd want to beat on something. What is it about really awful things—like traffic accidents—that you can't take your eyes away from them? I can't take my eyes off Junior.

Now I hear Miss Stern saying, "The show isn't quite over yet. There is one more ensemble to show you."

I tear my eyes away from the car wreck and look up at the stage, where an eighth-grader is standing next to Miss Stern. She turns slowly in place, just as all the other models did, but this time there's something different. She's not wearing a flowered skirt or a pastel top or a boxy jacket. This girl is wearing a bolero jacket in a wild pink color, a short grass-green dress with a puffy skirt, black leggings, and ballet flats. (I guess I have learned something from Alyce.)

Then Miss Stern beckons to someone backstage. Elwin comes out and stands next to the model.

"Everyone," Miss Stern says, "you are looking at an outfit that was designed by one of our very own students, Elwin Watt. Now, Elwin has never been in a sewing class here, but he came to me one day and said he wanted to become a clothing designer when he grows up and asked if he could join a sewing class. Well, that wasn't possible, so instead, Elwin came to the sewing room every afternoon, when school was out, and worked."

My eyes are pogoing up and down between Elwin on the stage and Junior down below with the band. The spotlight is on Elwin, and at first he blinks a little, then he looks down at his feet and smiles. There's a light on Junior's face, too. He's not smiling. And that light . . . He's texting or emailing. What is that rat up to?

"Elwin," Miss Stern is saying, "worked harder than any student I have ever taught. And he did something that no student has ever done before. Elwin didn't follow any ready-made pattern; he created his own. And this is the result."

The applause is wild. Elwin looks confused; Miss Stern has to tell him to take a bow.

Elwin's not the only one who's confused. I am,

too. I had everything all mixed up. I thought Miss Stern was just an old lady who was making my life miserable. But really, I was the one making her life miserable. She loves sewing. And I was a kid who hated sewing, hated the class, didn't even like her very much. It must have been pretty tough for her to have to face me every day. And then along came Elwin.

Callie's Rule:

- Scratch the rule about sewing assistants. Let's keep the sewing teachers. But they should only teach the kids who really, really, really like to sew.

Now Mr. No-Man bounds up the stairs to the stage and plants himself between Miss Stern and Elwin. He looks sort of dazed for a minute, then he pastes a fake smile across his face, and he says, "I have one more announcement to make this evening. I've seen the stupendous effort Elwin made to learn to sew and to design clothing. And as I was sitting here, this evening, among all of you proud friends and parents, I came to a very important realization."

It's amazing how many of Mr. No-Man's sentences begin with "I."

"I realized that there may well be other talented boys at our school, boys who should not be denied the opportunity that Elwin has had. And so I have decided to make the sewing classes not a requirement but an elective, open to both boys and girls. Now this will take a fair amount of work on my part, rescheduling and so forth, but I am more than willing to make the effort if other boys, following Elwin's pioneering effort, are enabled to start down the path to achieving their dreams."

A bit of applause here, mostly from the girls, who now realize they won't have to take sewing again, but then the clapping grows louder—I think more for Elwin's "pioneering effort" than for anything Mr. No-Man said. But he's standing there, ducking his head in a half bow, as if he wasn't the one who said no to Elwin's idea in the first place. As if he wasn't the one who thought up a hundred and fifty reasons why boys *shouldn't* take sewing.

It wasn't his idea; it was mine. I should be

taking that bow right now. No, Mr. Nolan had nothing to do with this. But Elwin did. The idea was mine, but Elwin did all the hard work. And I think, maybe, just maybe, Mr. No-Man knows that. And I hope that maybe he'll stop thinking of me as a troublemaker and maybe think that I had something to do with all that applause he's getting right now.

Junior seems to have switched off his phone; I can't see his face. But Mr. No-Man is reaching into his pocket, taking out his own phone and reading something.

"May I have your attention, please," he says, looking angry. "I've just gotten an email claiming that a bomb has been set to go off in ten minutes. Now, I'm sure that this is merely a misguided prank, but it would be best not to take any chances. There is no need to panic, but I'd like you all to please leave through the side exits."

A fake bomb scare? Junior, it was Junior. Junior emailed that message. He couldn't stand that Elwin was up there taking a bow. Junior wanted to ruin it for Elwin. But it turns out he didn't ruin anything. Everyone's leaving, but they're taking their time, chatting, walking slowly. They know the bomb threat was a fake. Like Junior. But Elwin's no fake. He got his applause. And Junior just got angry.

In the morning, Alyce and I sit down to write the story for *The Hawke*. This is what we write:

> The Hillcrest Middle School fashion show, held on Monday night, was a great success. Half the girls at the school—all of those who had taken sewing in the spring semester—participated, modeling the garments they had spent so much time and effort on.

There's a paragraph next about what the girls were wearing. Alyce has a lot to say about that.

> Contributing to the success of the evening was the school band, which played continuously throughout the show. Like the girls, the band spent many weeks rehearsing. Some of the band members played a double role, modeling their fashions as well.

Those double roles involved a great deal of rushing from the front of the auditorium to the stage and back.

> The art classes contributed also, designing posters and programs for the event.
>
> On the night of the show, the auditorium was filled with proud family members and friends. Their enthusiasm was loud and hearty.
>
> At the end of the evening, everyone who had worked on the show took their bows alongside the models. There was loud applause for all of them.
>
> But perhaps the loudest applause of all came at the end, when Miss Stern introduced Elwin Watt and a model displayed the original outfit Elwin had designed and made himself.

I'm back and forth about putting in a line about Mr. Nolan deciding that sewing should be open to both boys and girls. One minute I don't want to give him credit, and the next minute I think that if

I put it out there, online, he won't be able to back down. So I do put it in.

> As a final note to the evening, Principal Nolan announced that because of Elwin's extraordinary effort, beginning in the fall, sewing would be an elective class open to both boys and girls.

There! Well done, Callie. You got Mr. No-Man's promise in writing, but you also gave all the credit to Elwin. And not one word about the bomb scare.

There's one more thing, something I don't put into my article, a rule:

Callie's Rule:

- They don't shine the spotlight on the person who's like everyone else. They shine it on the person who stands out.

I just got a new email—from Mr. Fischer!

To all the e-reporters,
    You all, individually and as a group, have accomplished

a great deal this year. I hope that, even though I won't be advising you, you'll continue writing.

Just remember to keep me posted. I want to read every issue.

James Fischer

Yes, Mr. Fischer, we will keep on writing, and we will keep you posted. All of us. The entire group.